I Could Be...
MINDFUL

A Coloring Book for All Ages

By Gia Pisto-Reade

Now let me see...

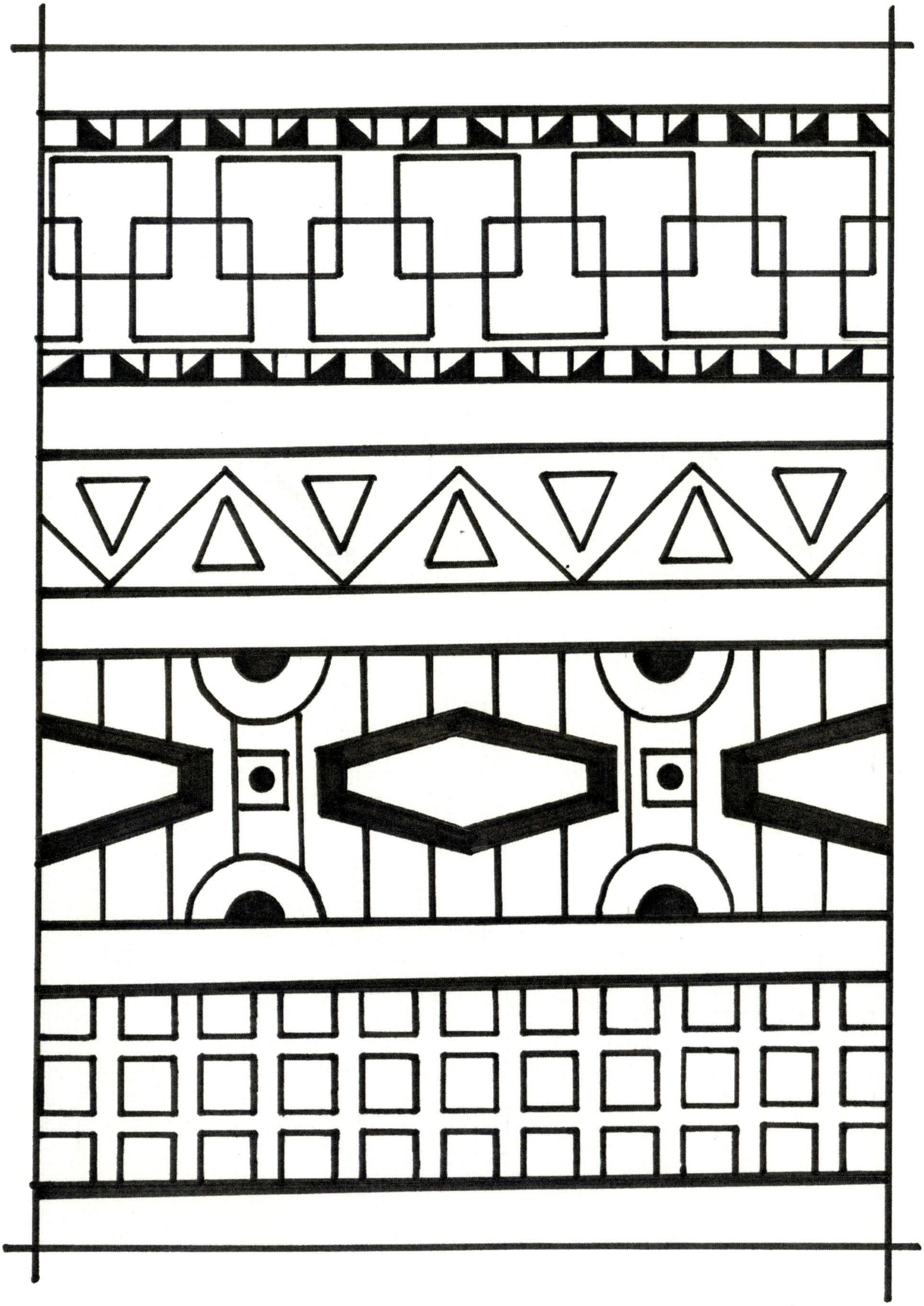

...what I could be.

I could be anything...

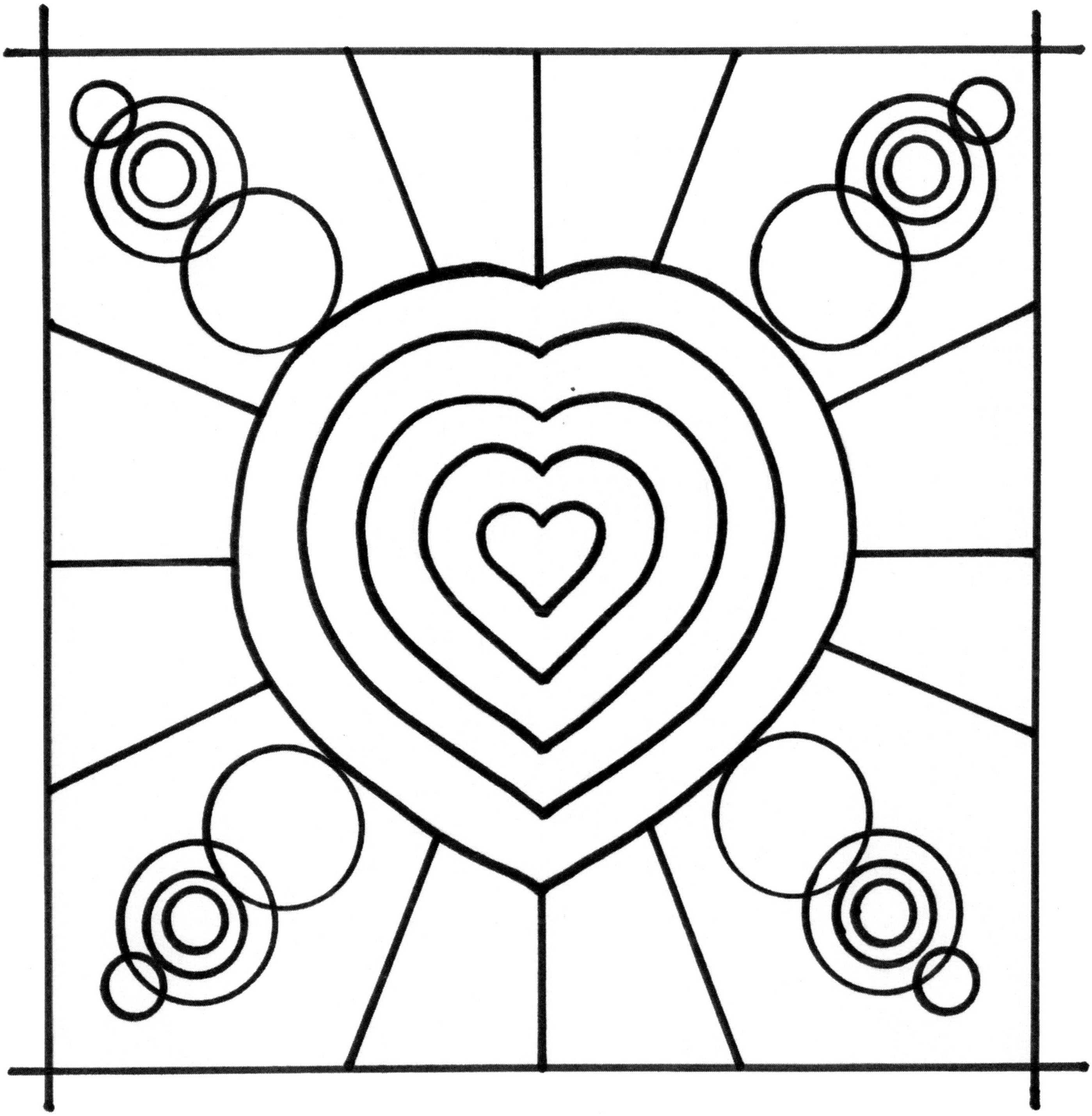

...that might make my heart sing!

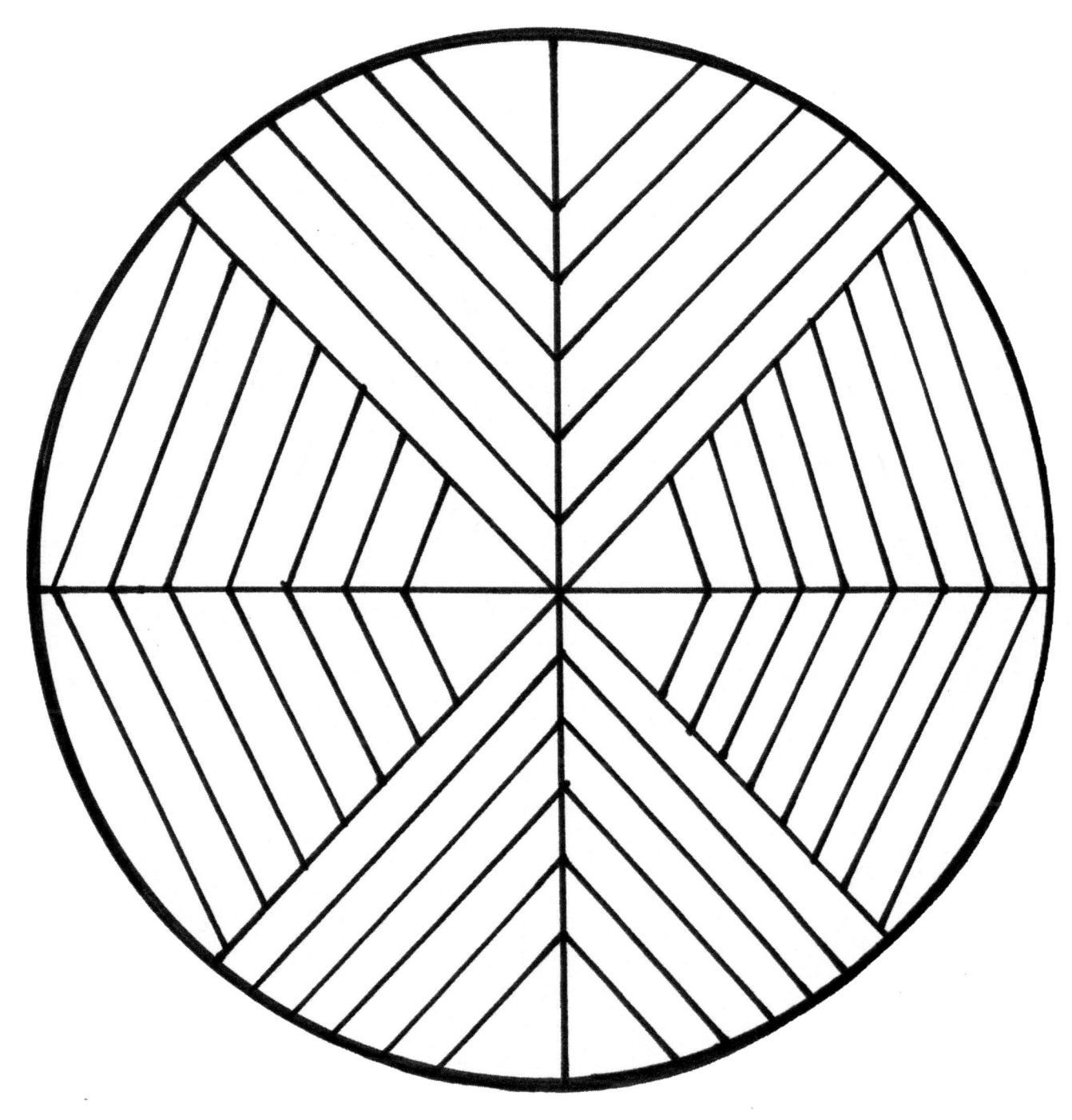

When I can't catch my breath...

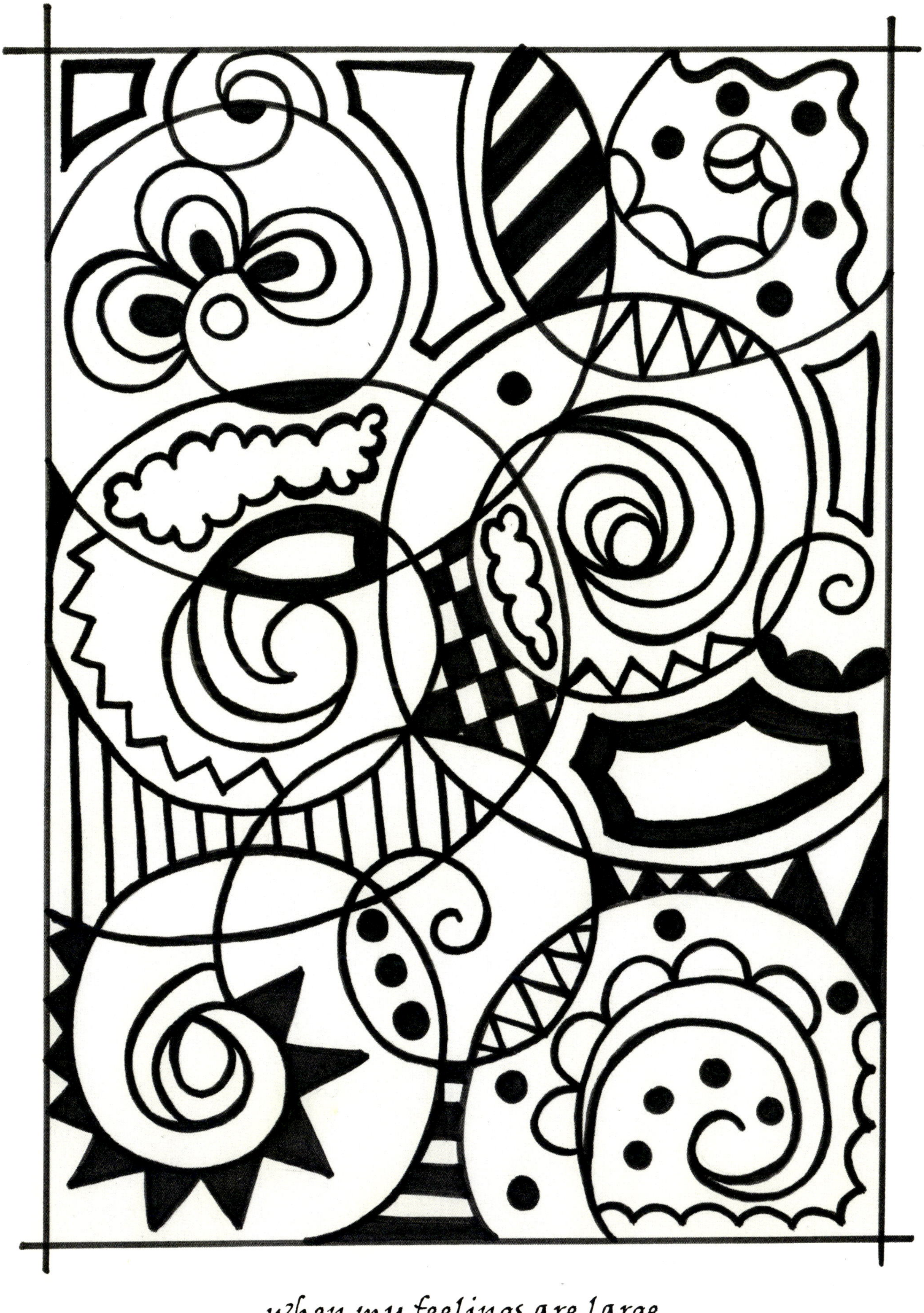

...when my feelings are large...

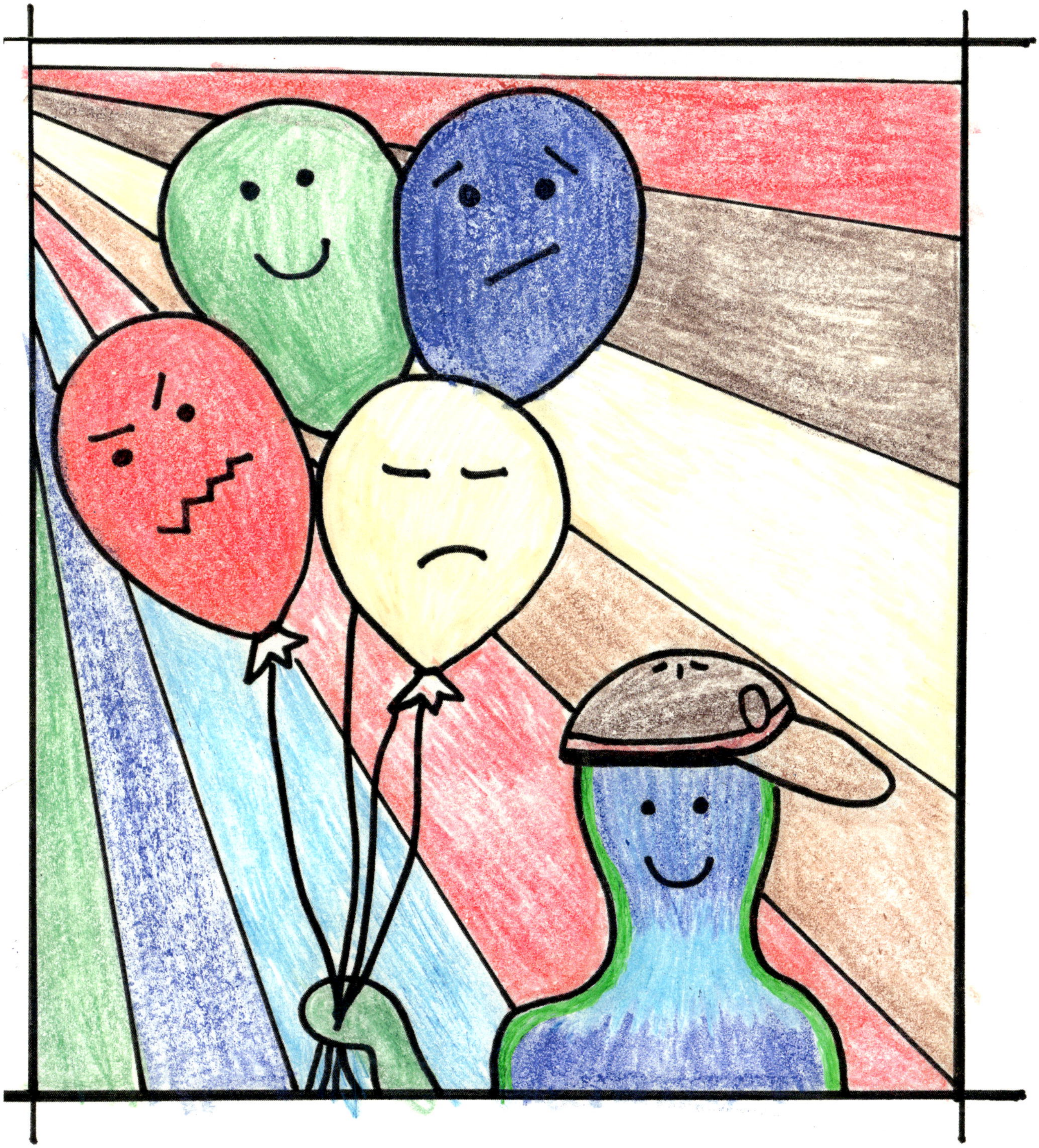

...when my body is lost...

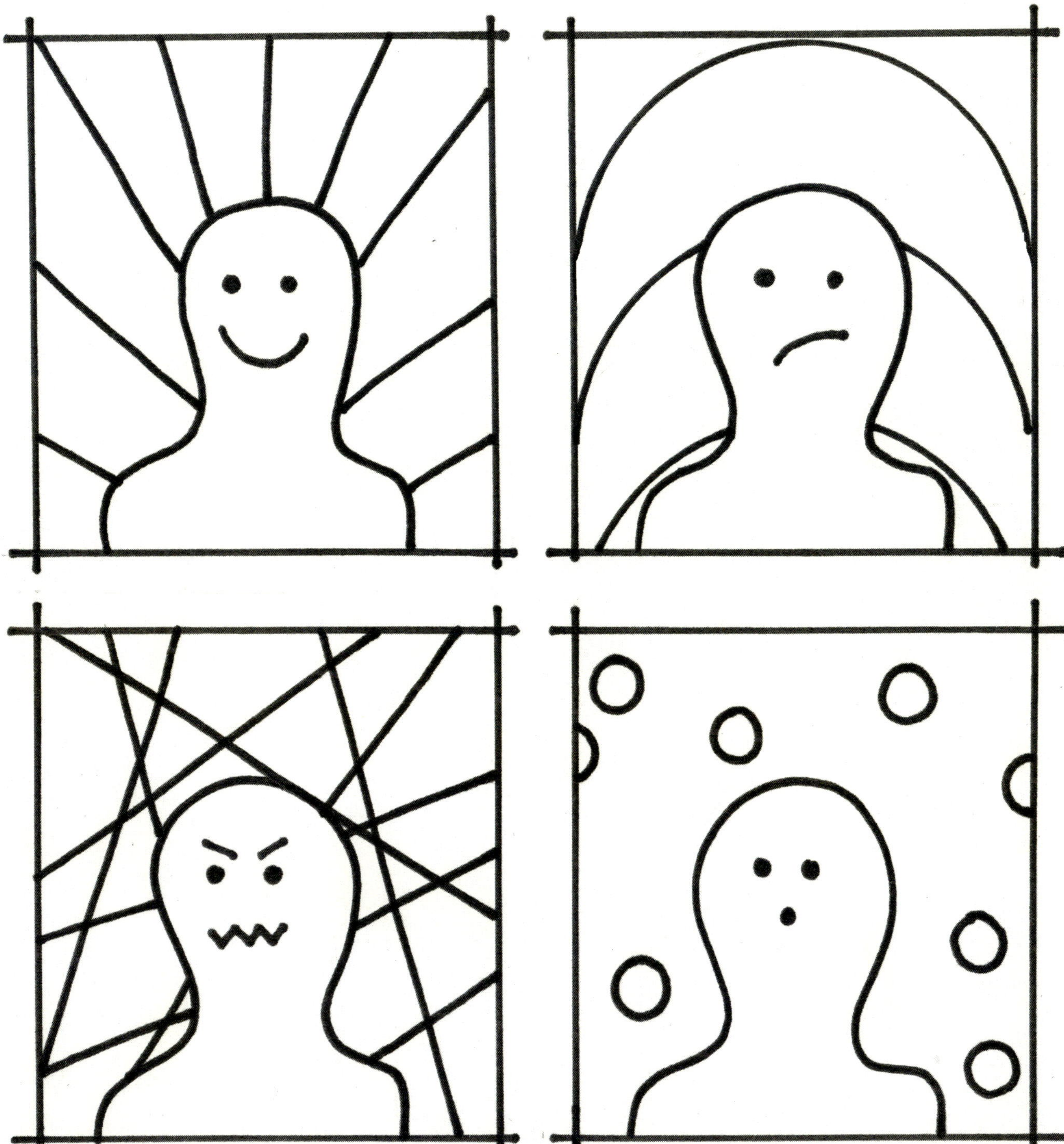

...emotions are in charge.

I have to remember...

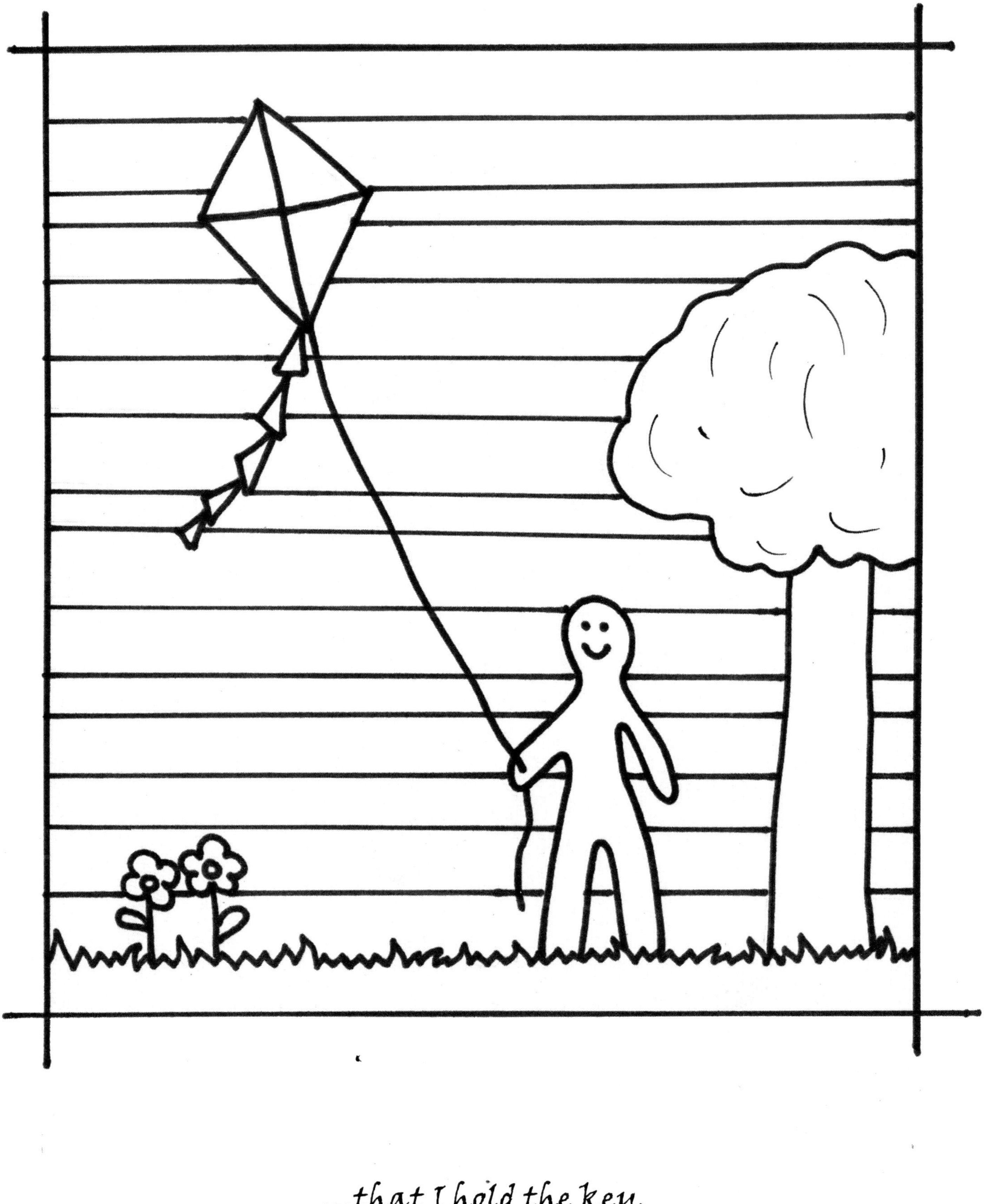

...that I hold the key.

The key is called Mindfulness...

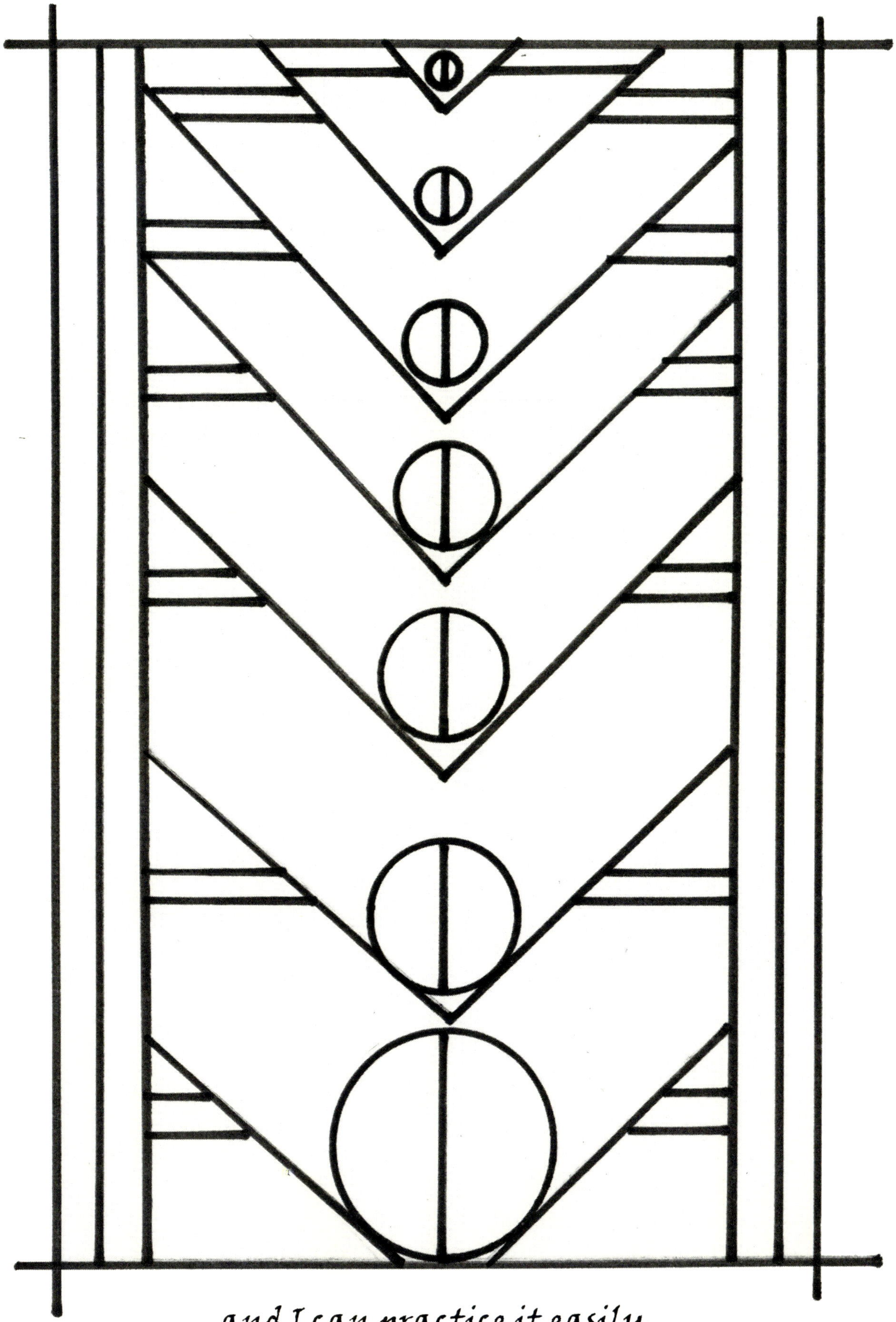

...and I can practice it easily.

I am a mountain...

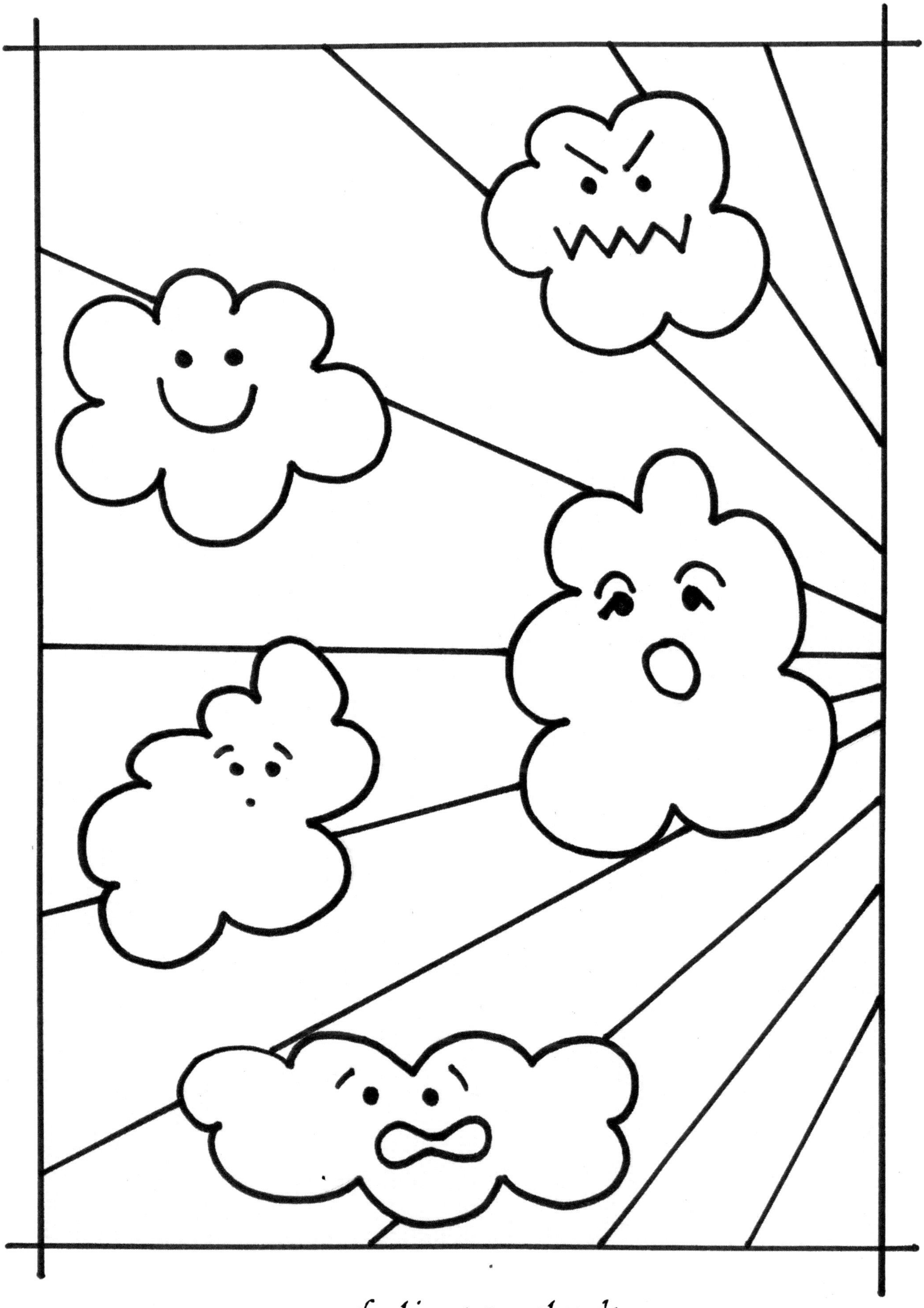

...my feelings are clouds.

Nothing gets in...

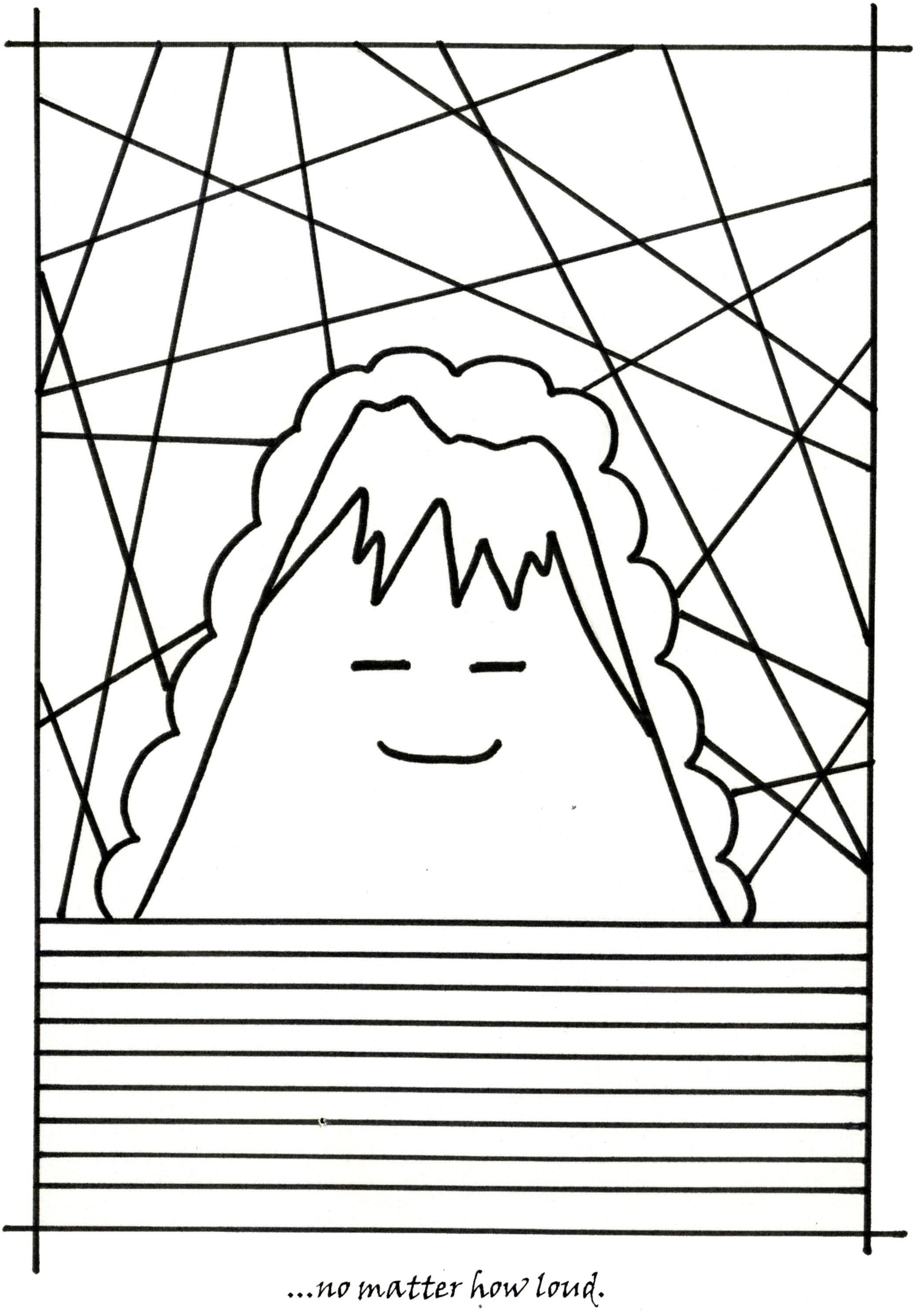

...no matter how loud.

I am a surfer...

...and waves are emotions.

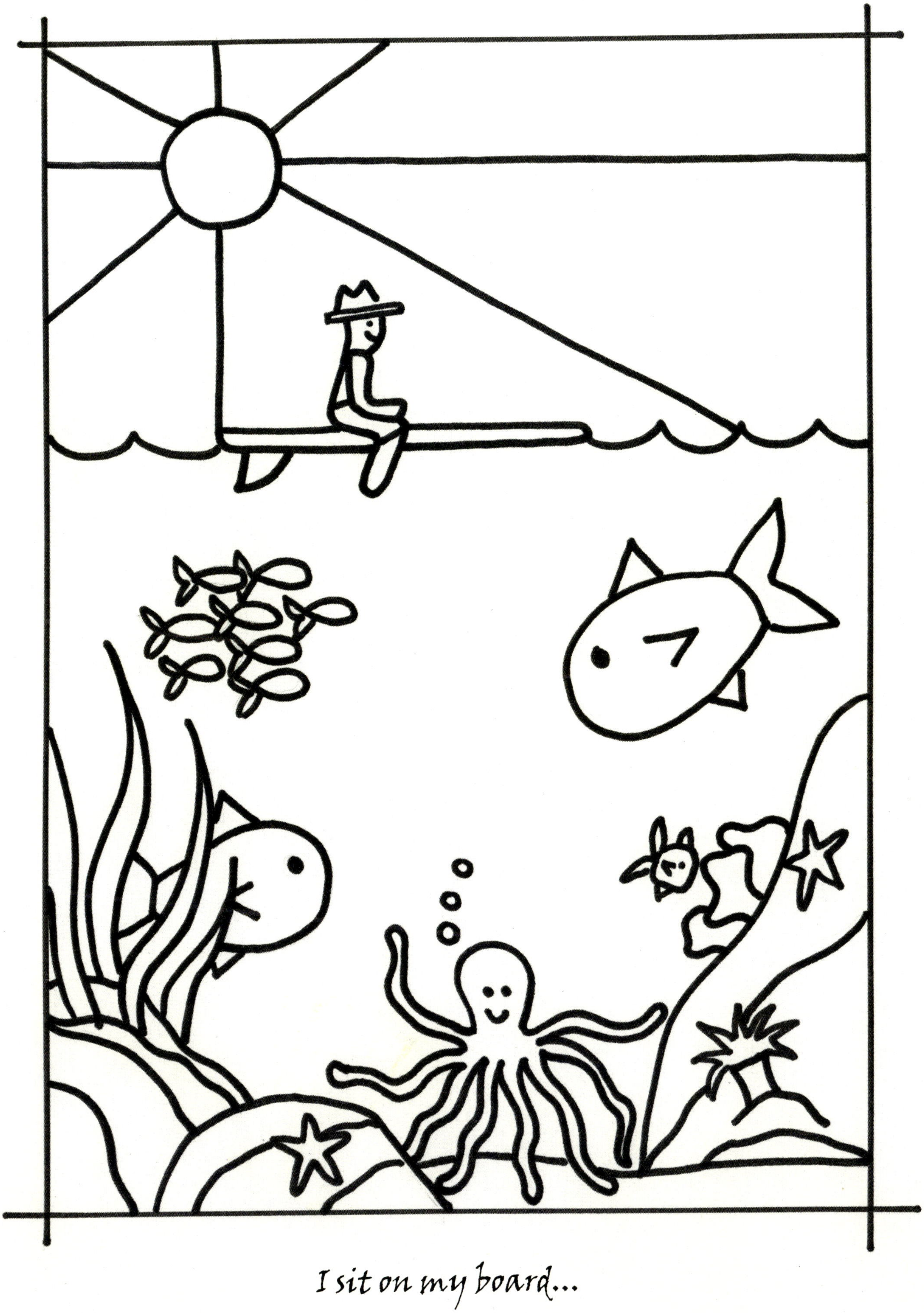

I sit on my board...

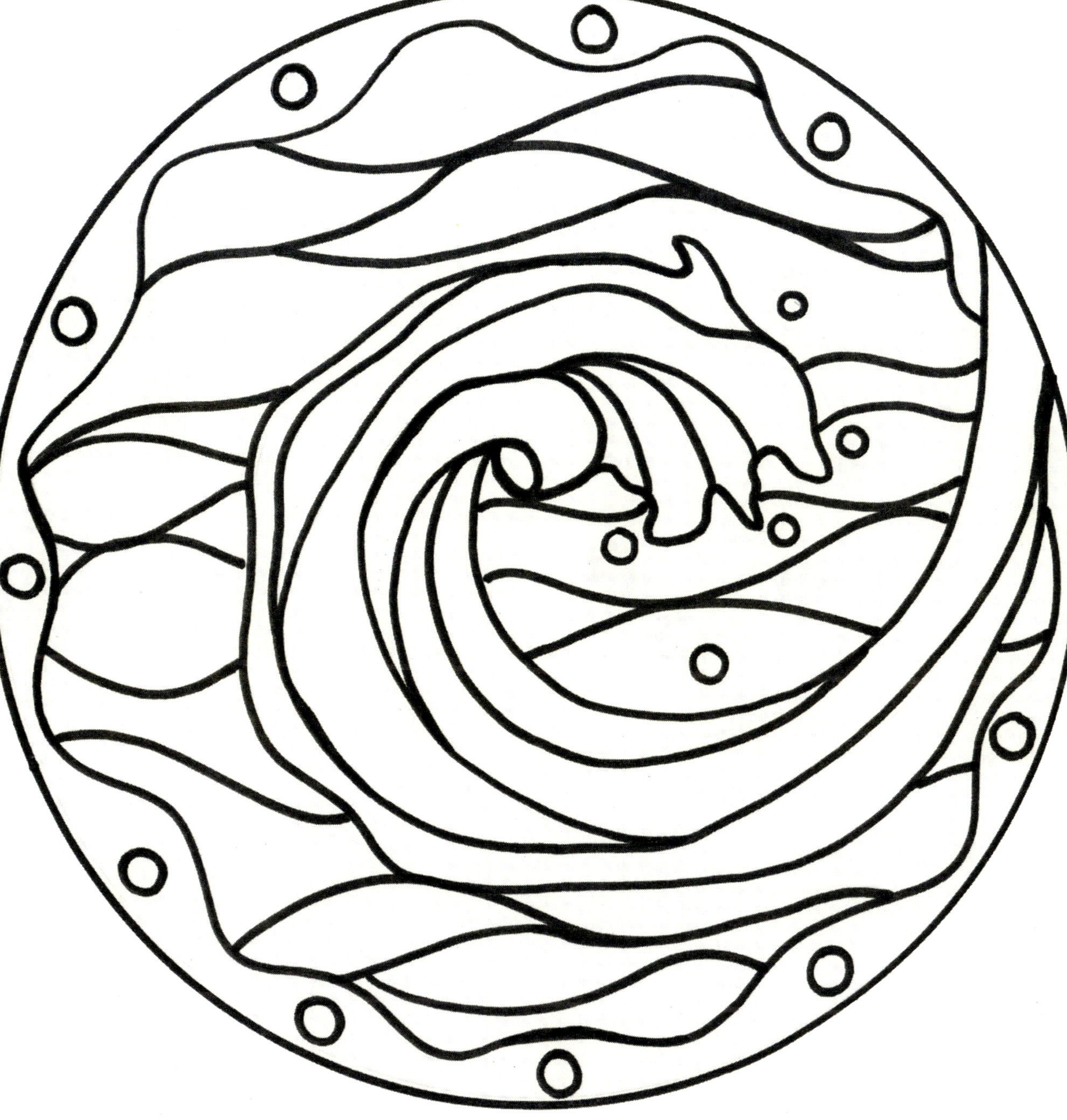

...calmly observing the commotion.

I am a star...

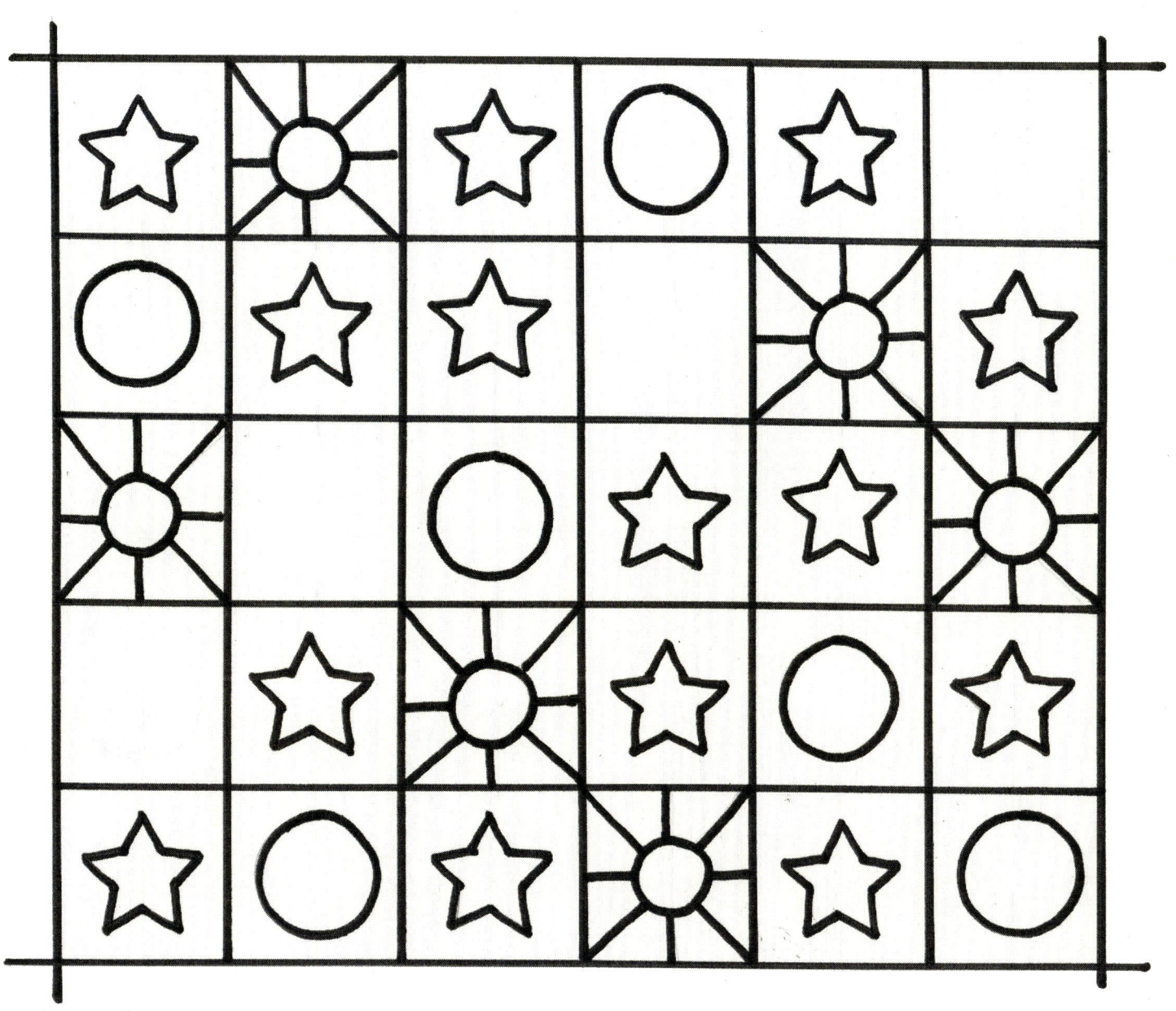

...one of many with the name.

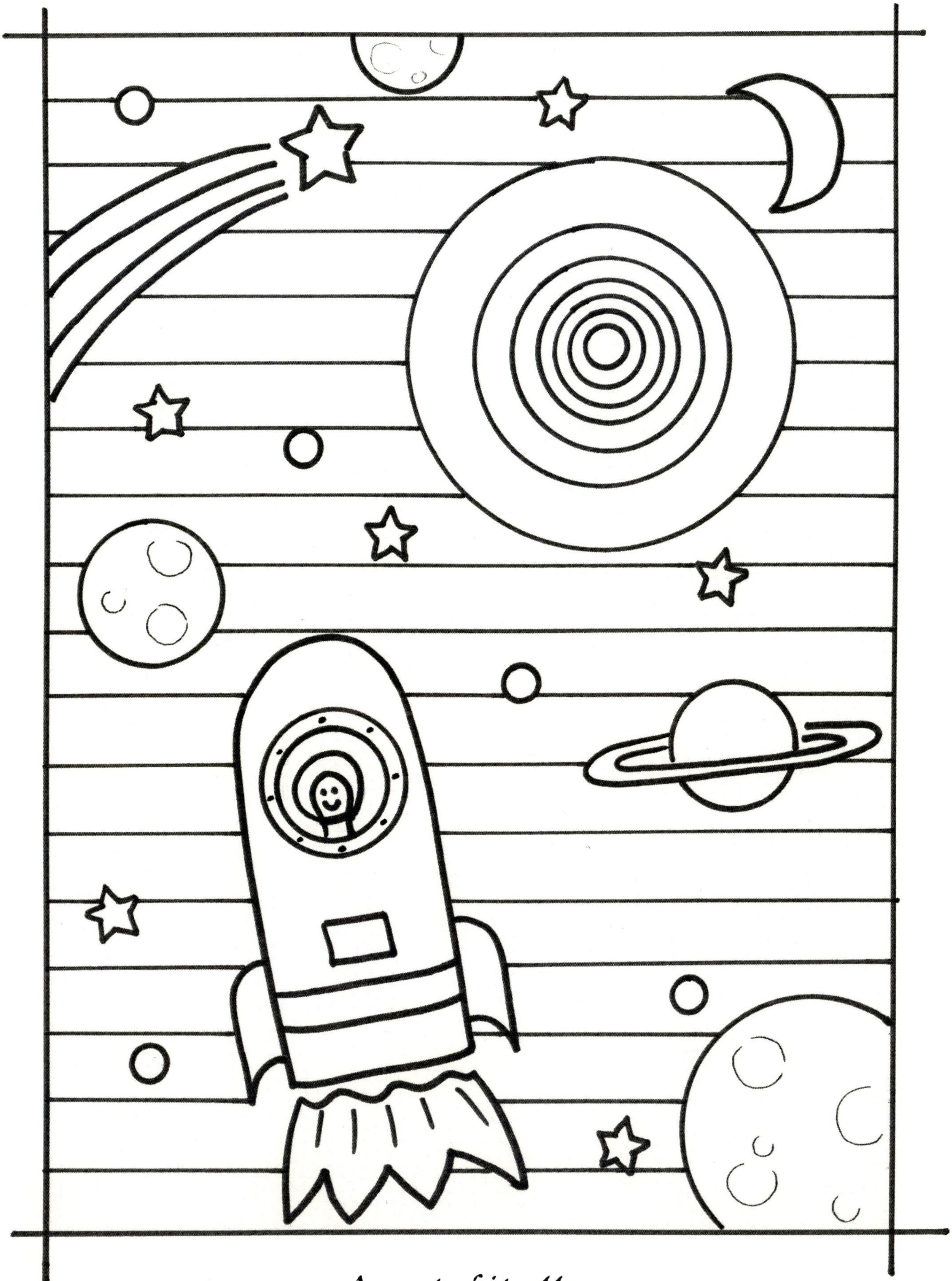

A part of it all...

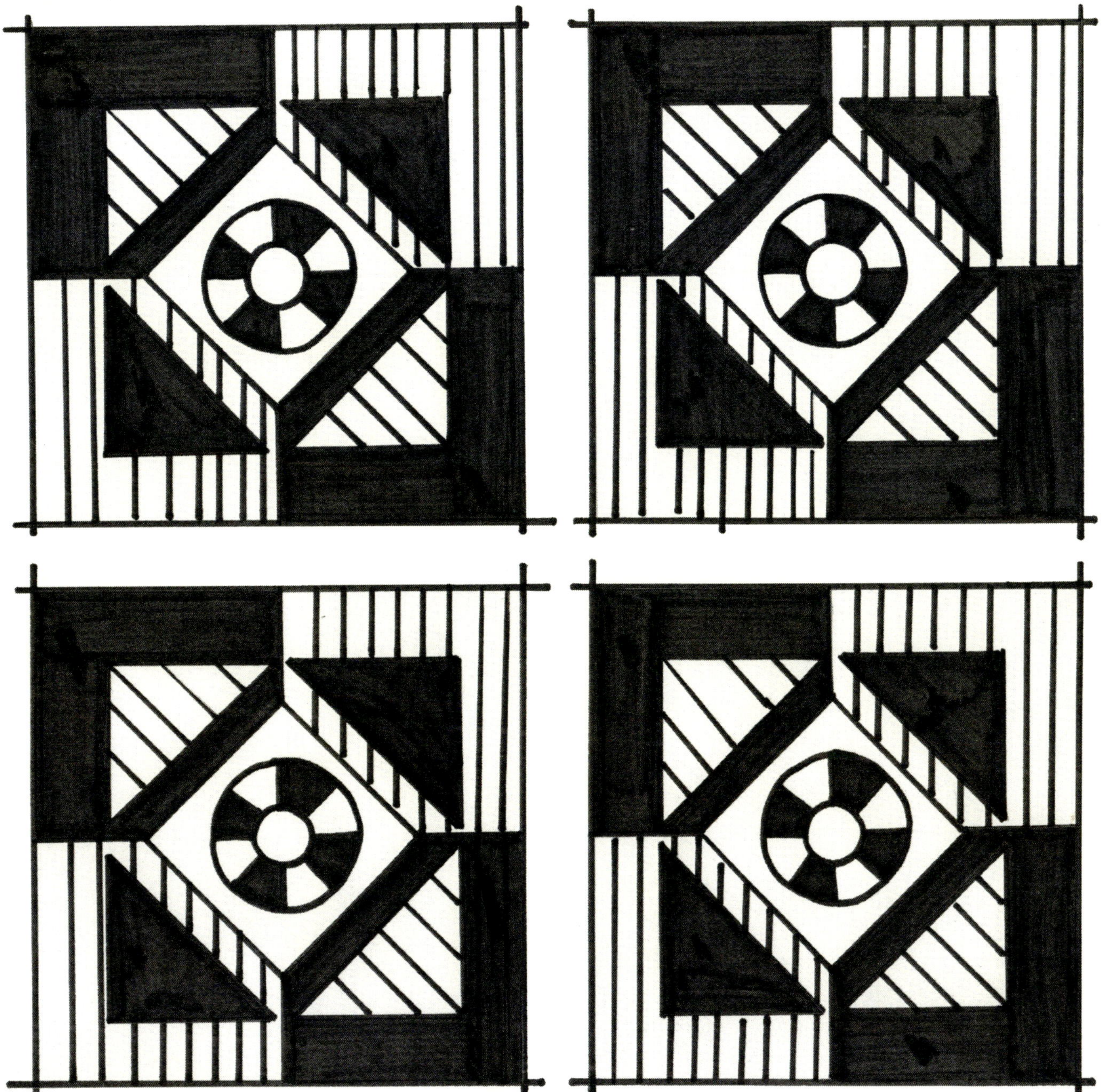

...all different, all the same.

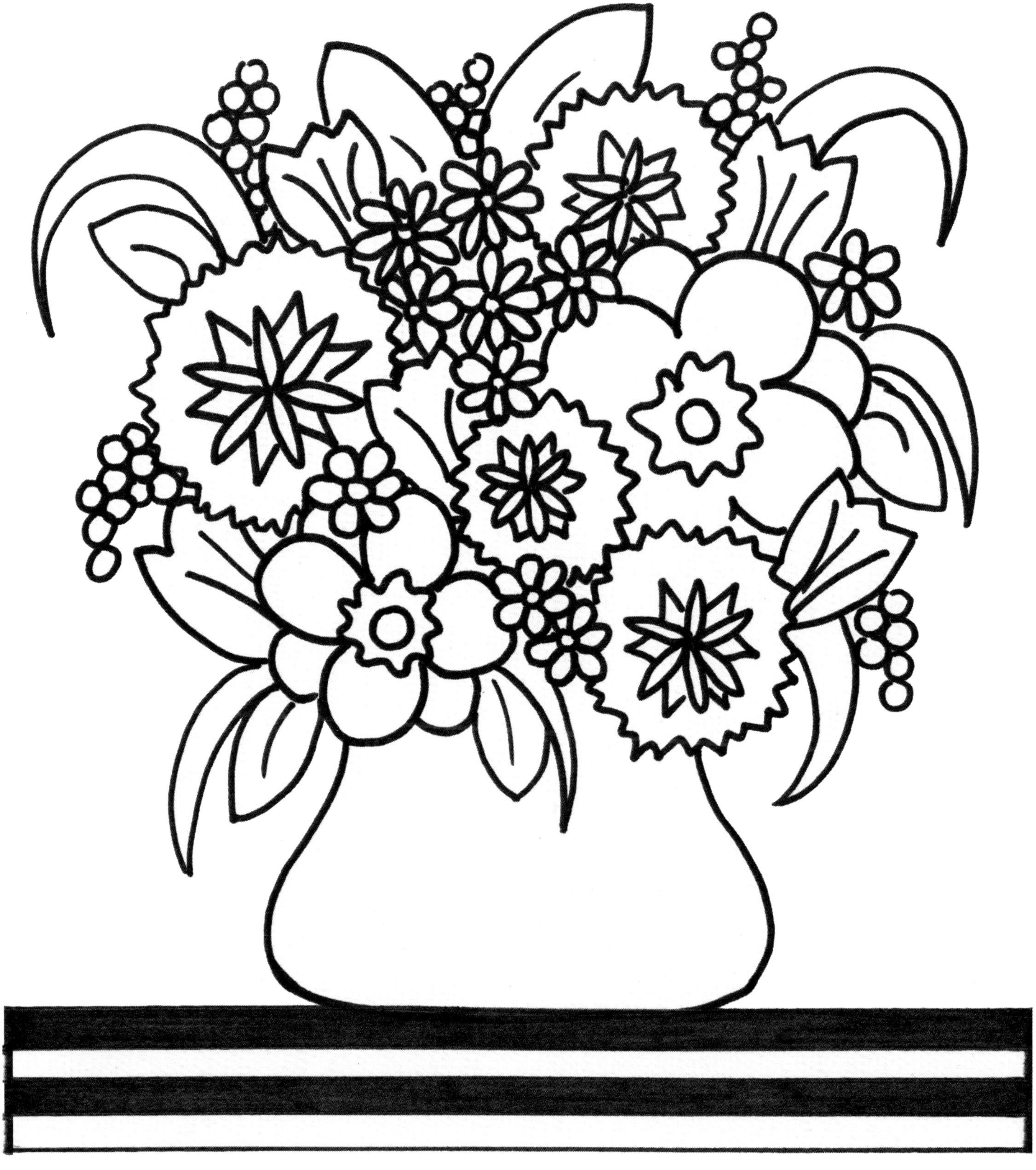

I am a flower...

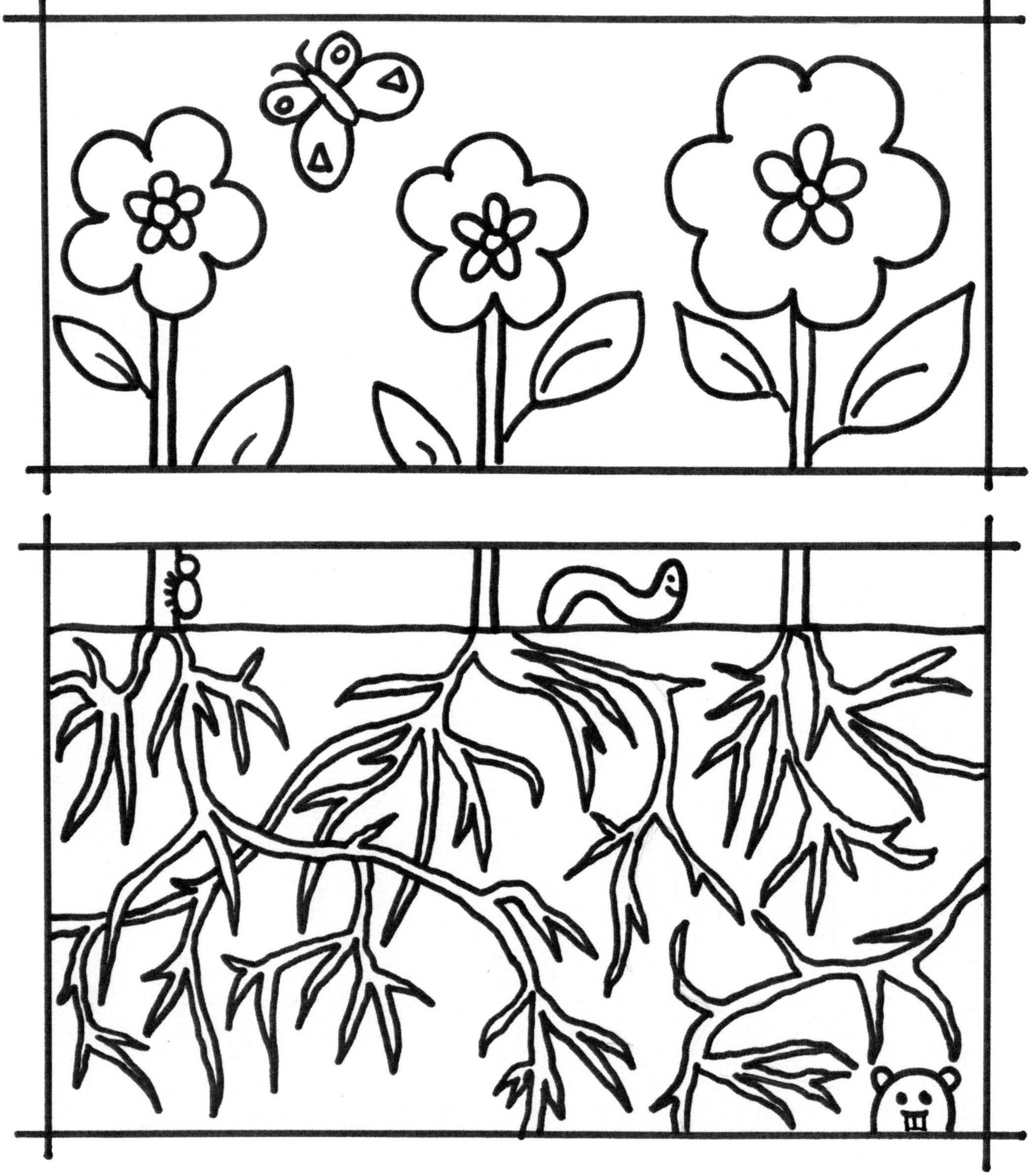

...with roots deep in the dirt.

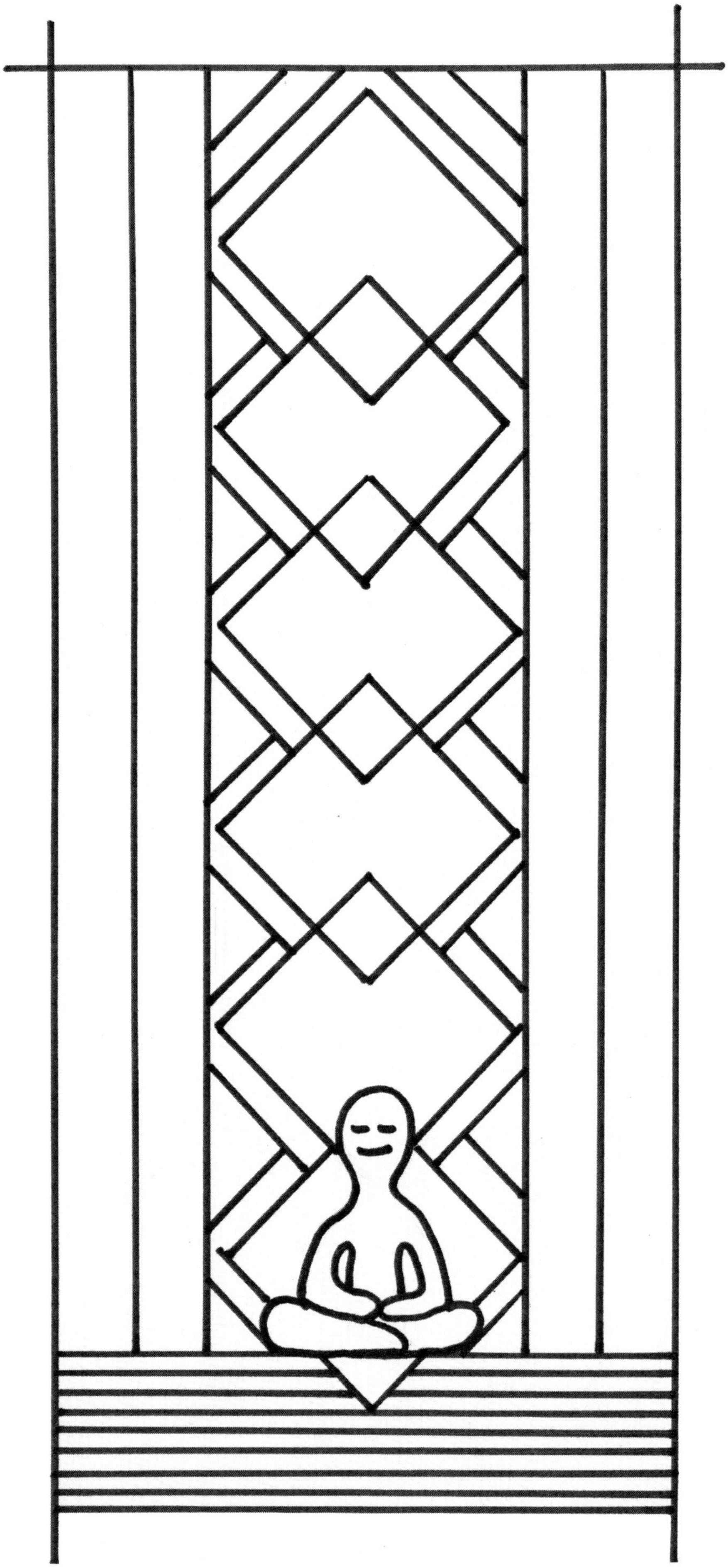

My energy is grounded...

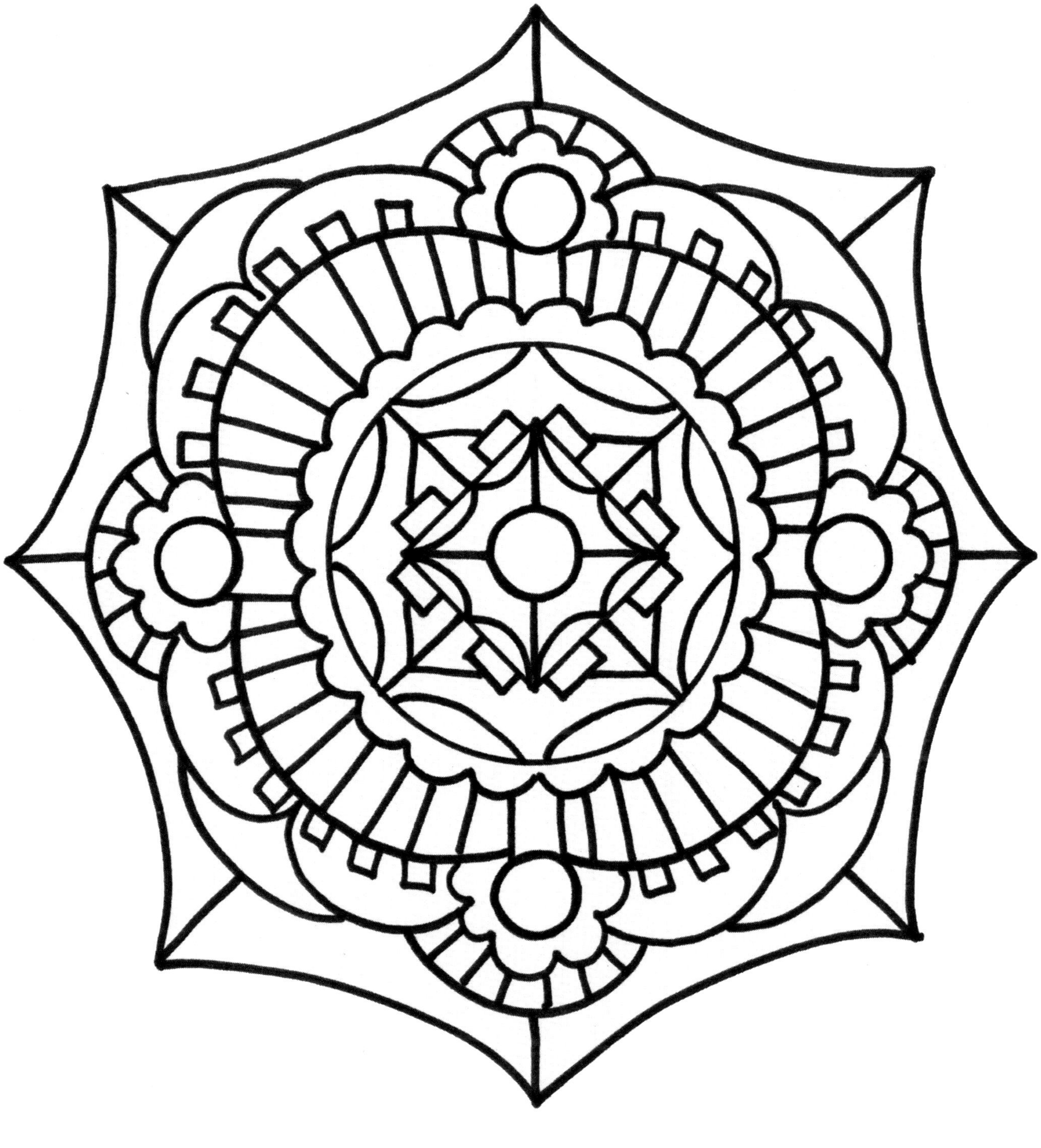

...so I feel no hurt.

I am an octopus...

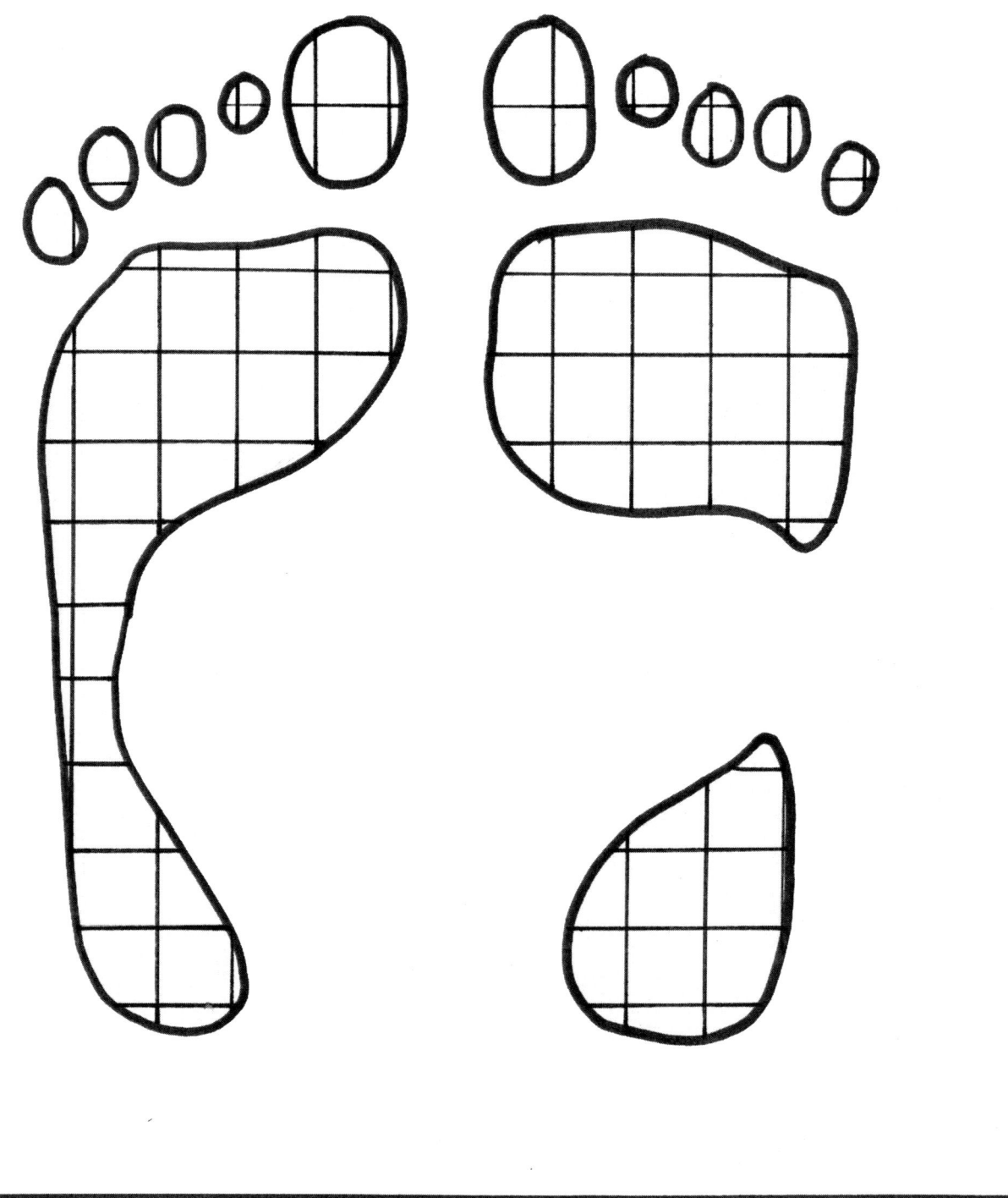

...I have sticky feet.

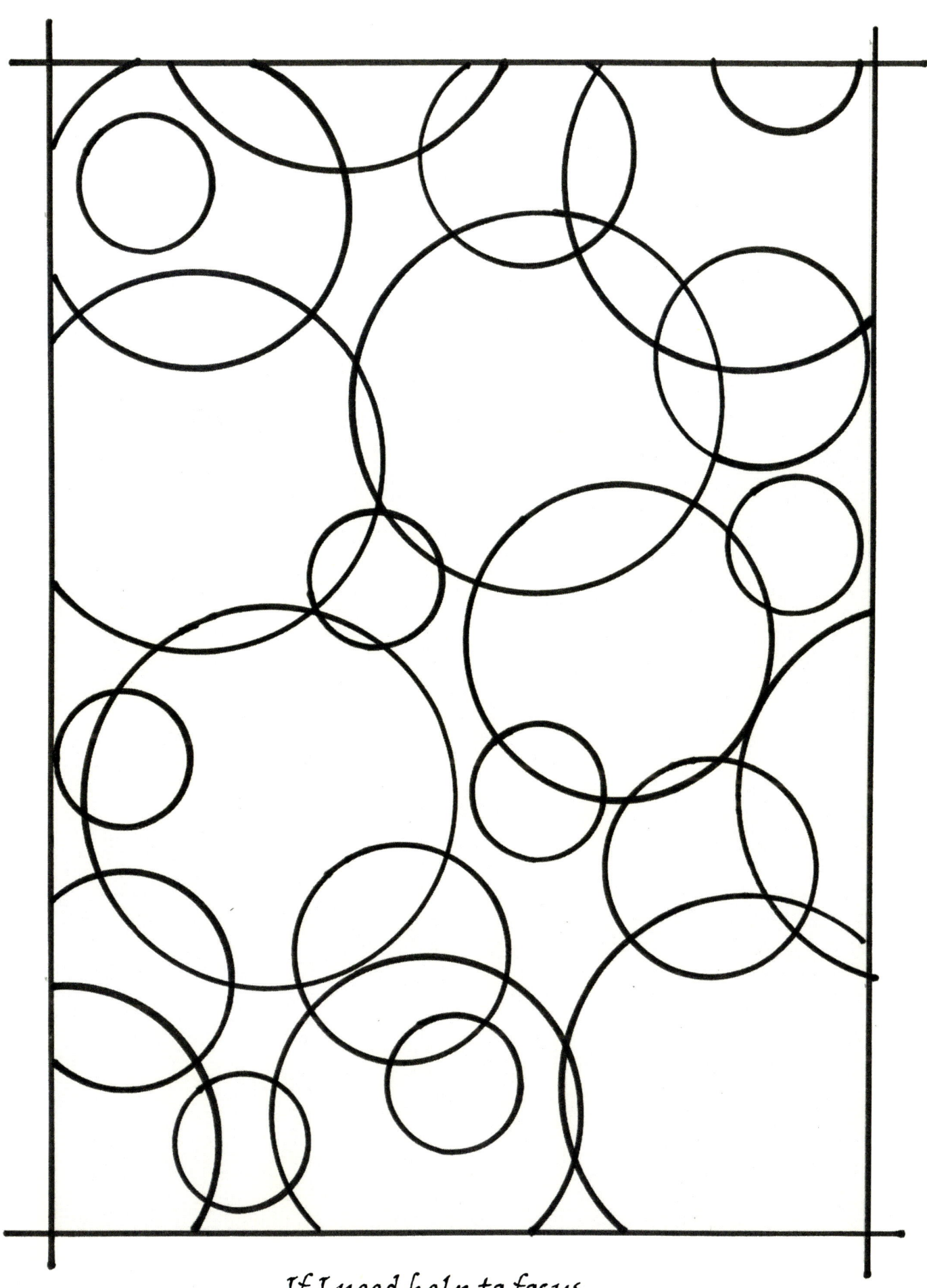

If I need help to focus...

...I feel them stick to the street.

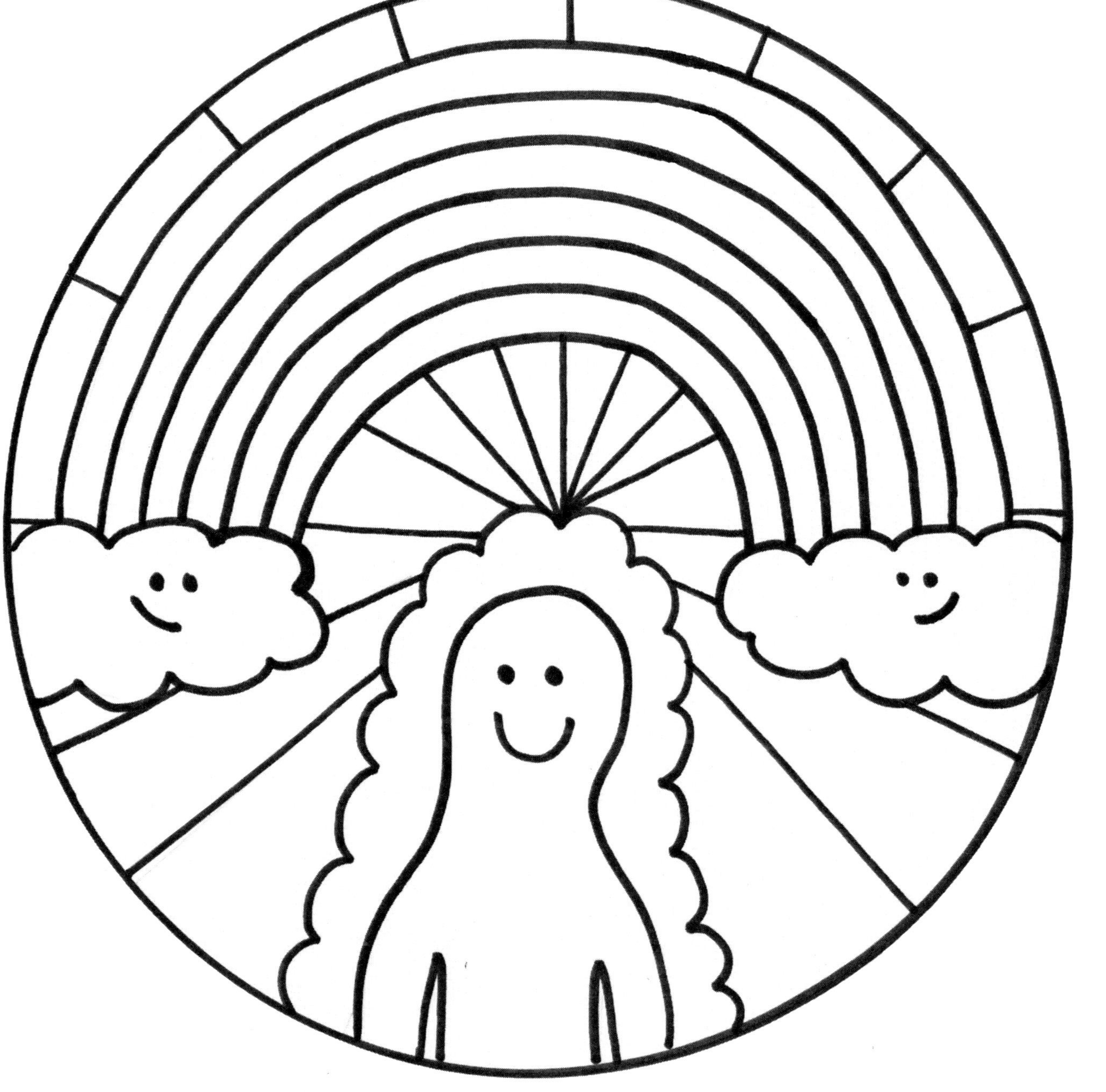

I am a rainbow...

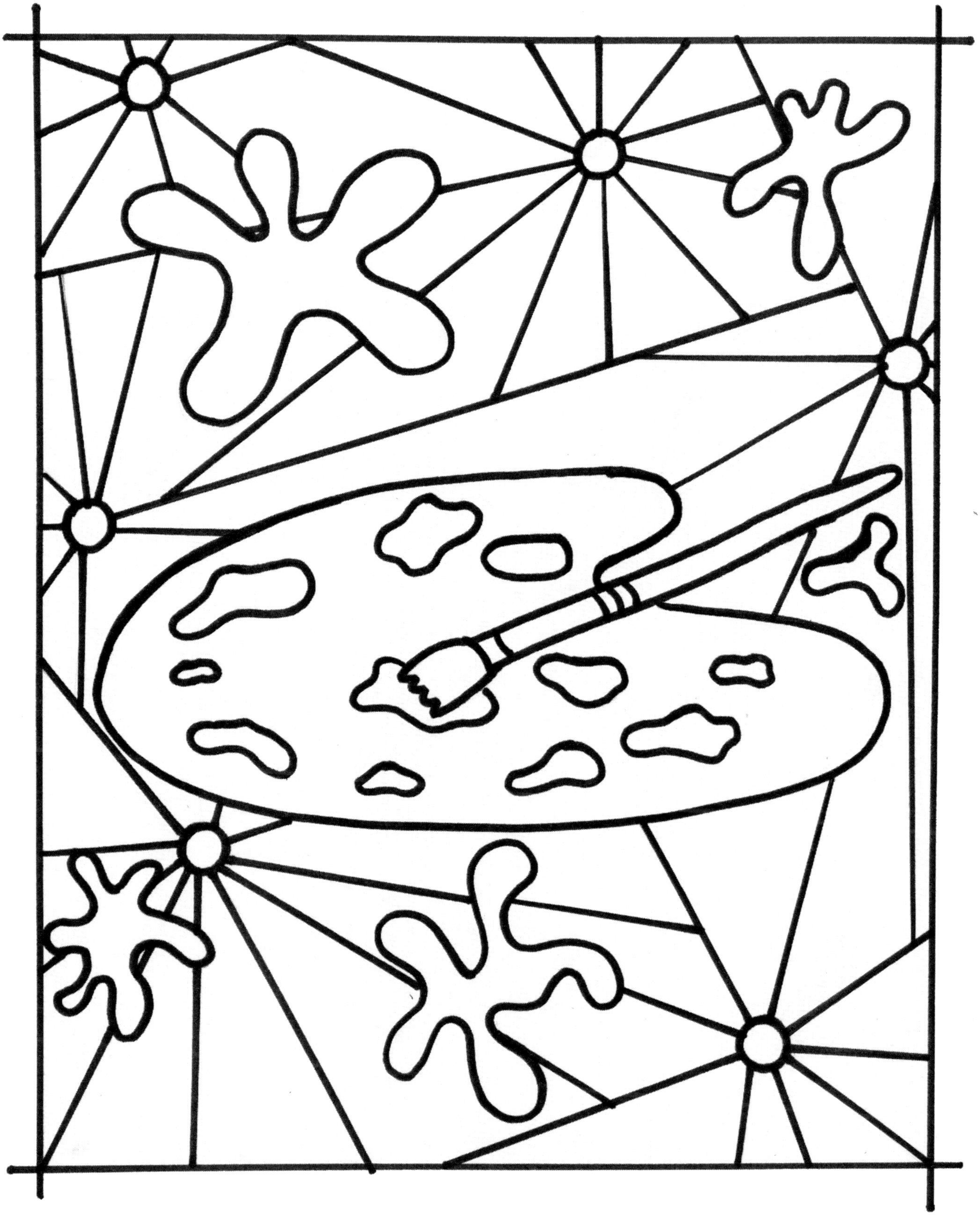

...I have all the colors.

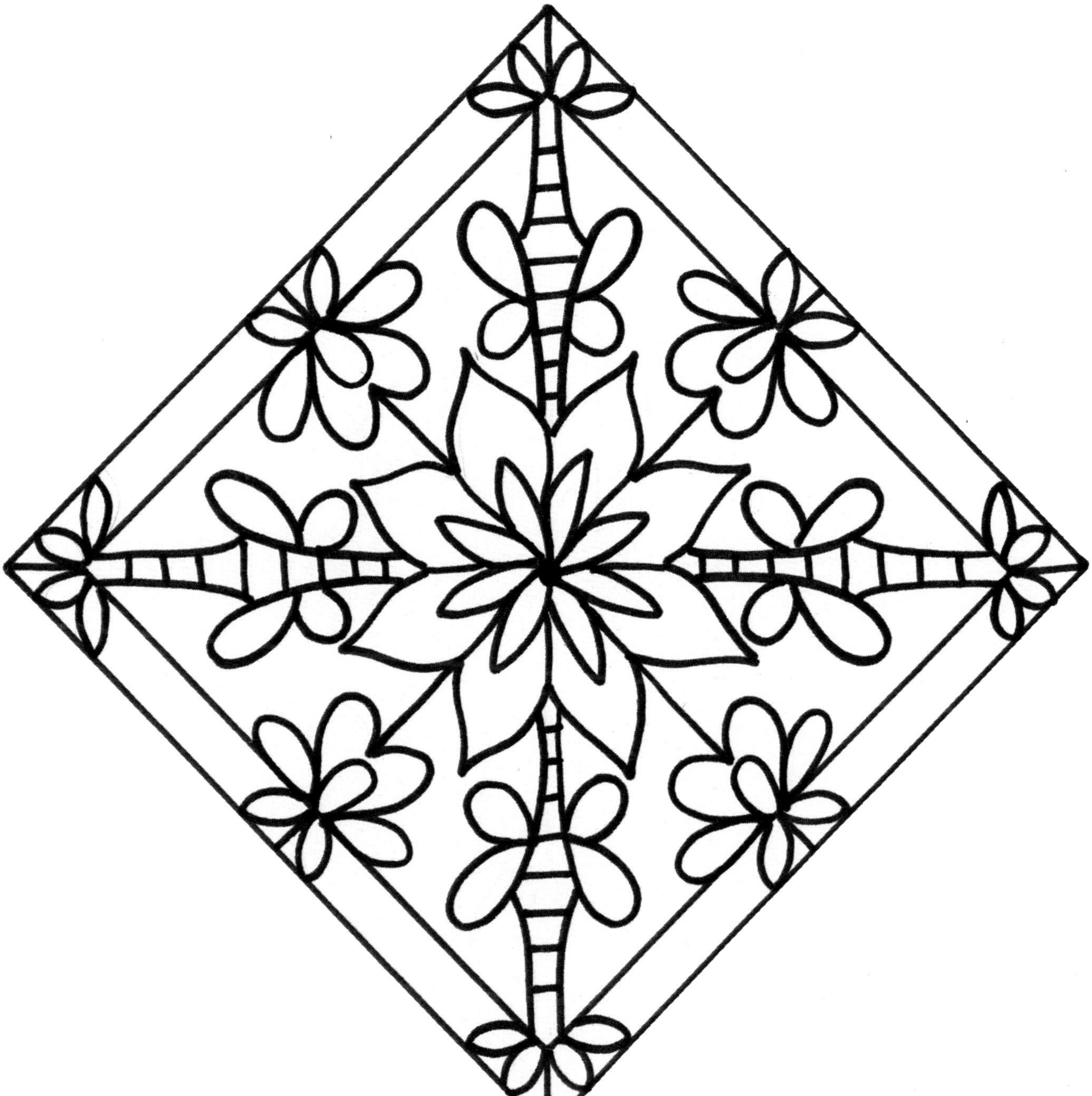

With sunshine in my heart...

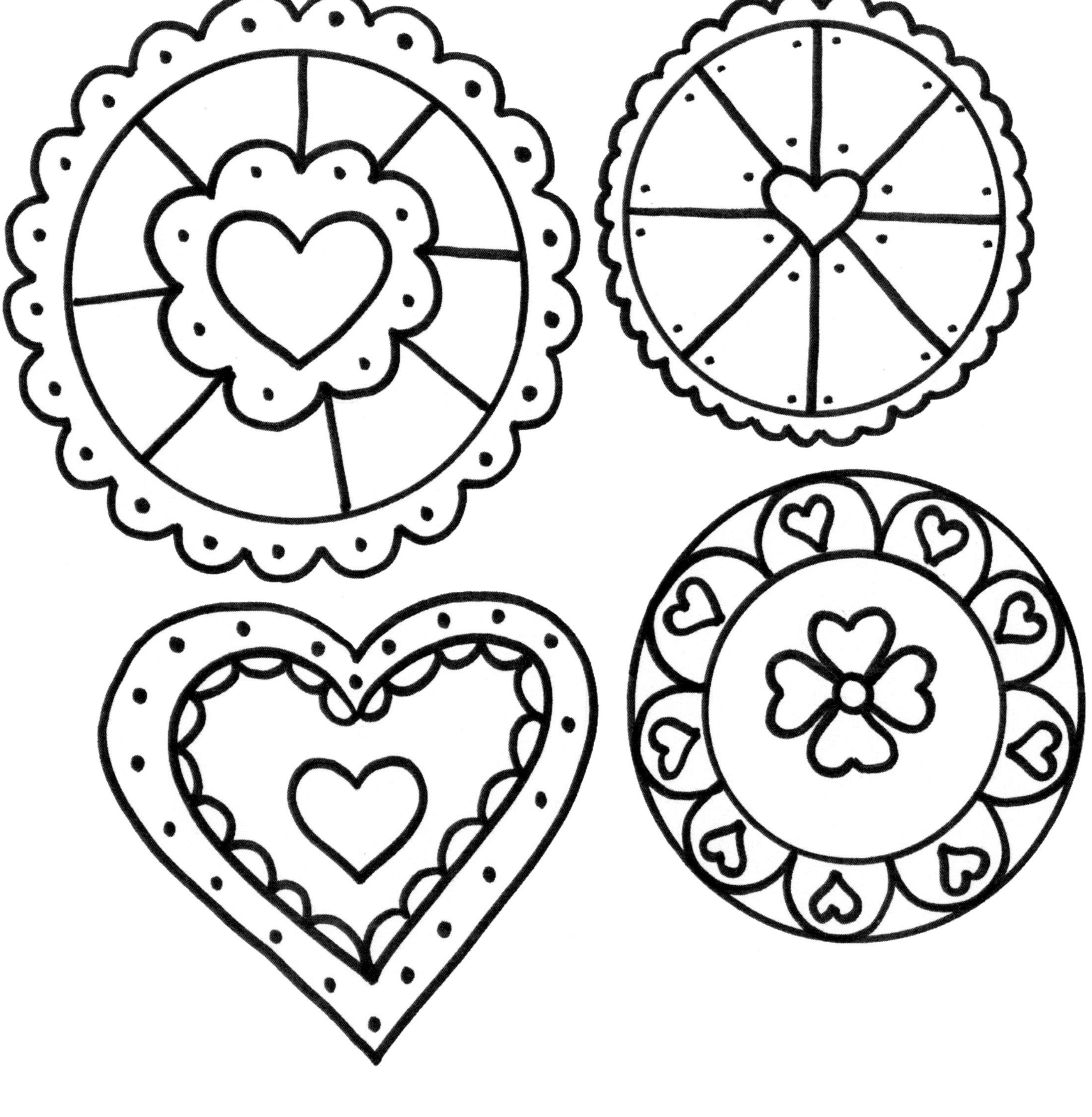

...I love myself and others.

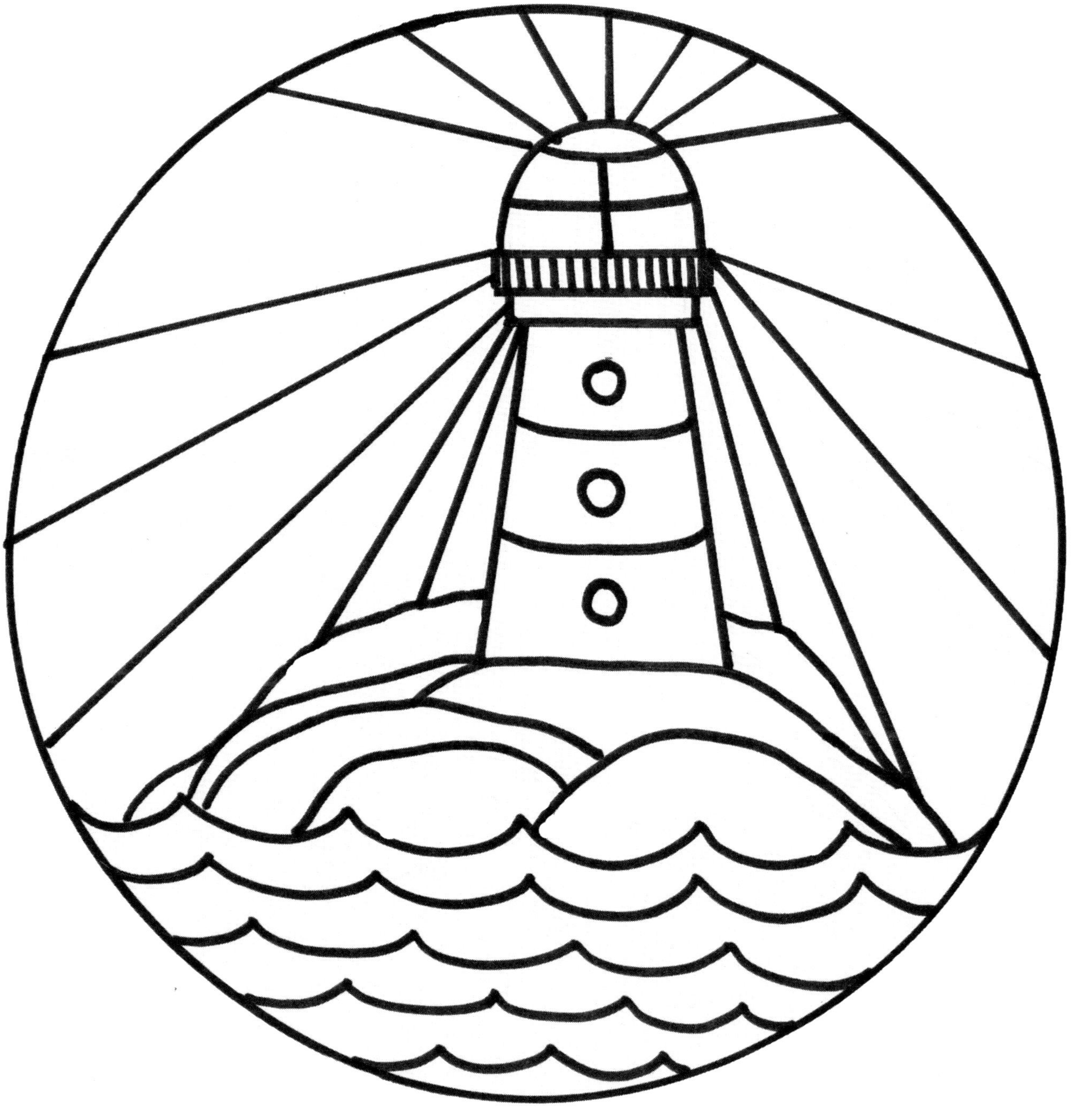

I am a lighthouse...

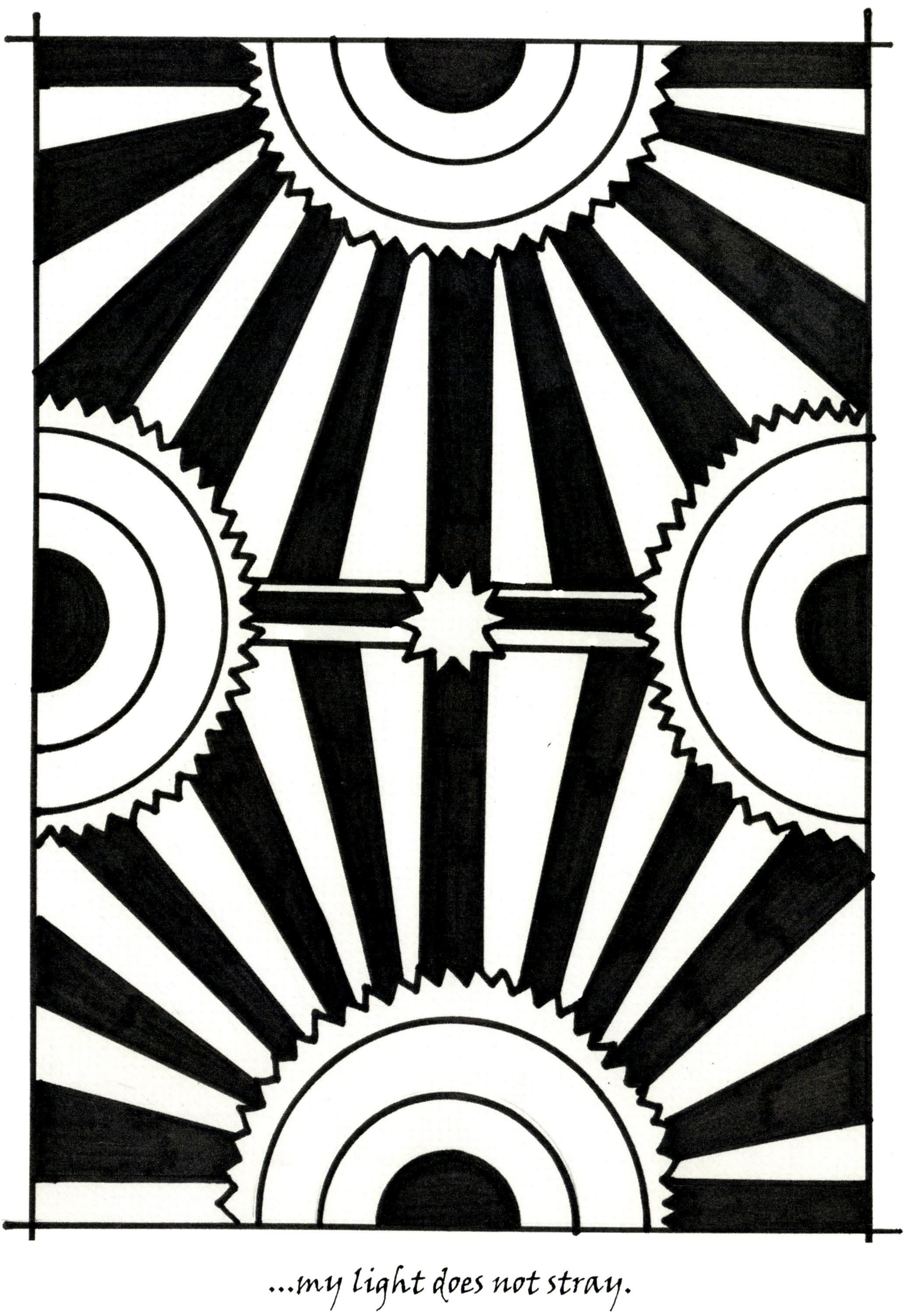

...my light does not stray.

The waves pound on my rocks...

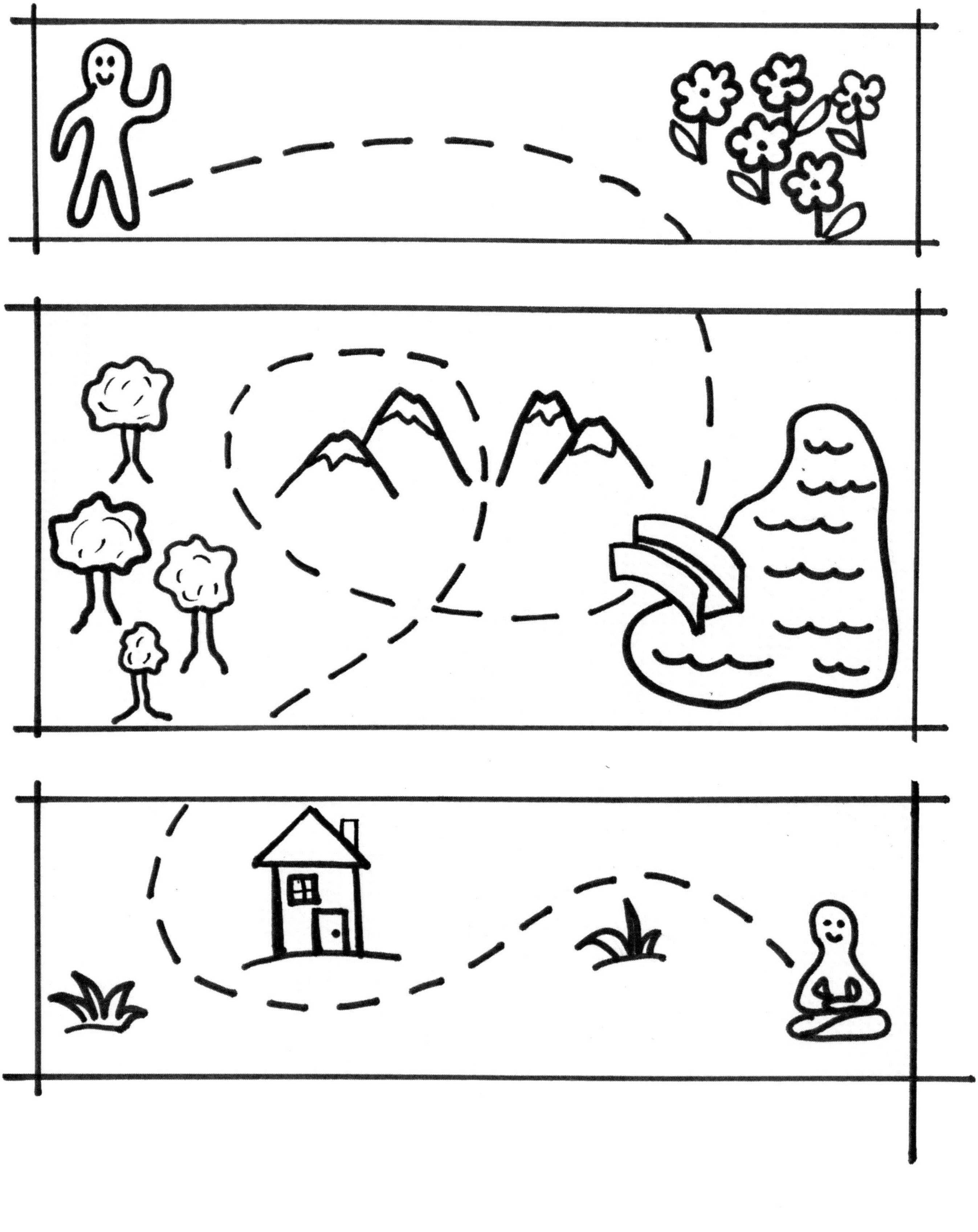

...but I can always find the way.

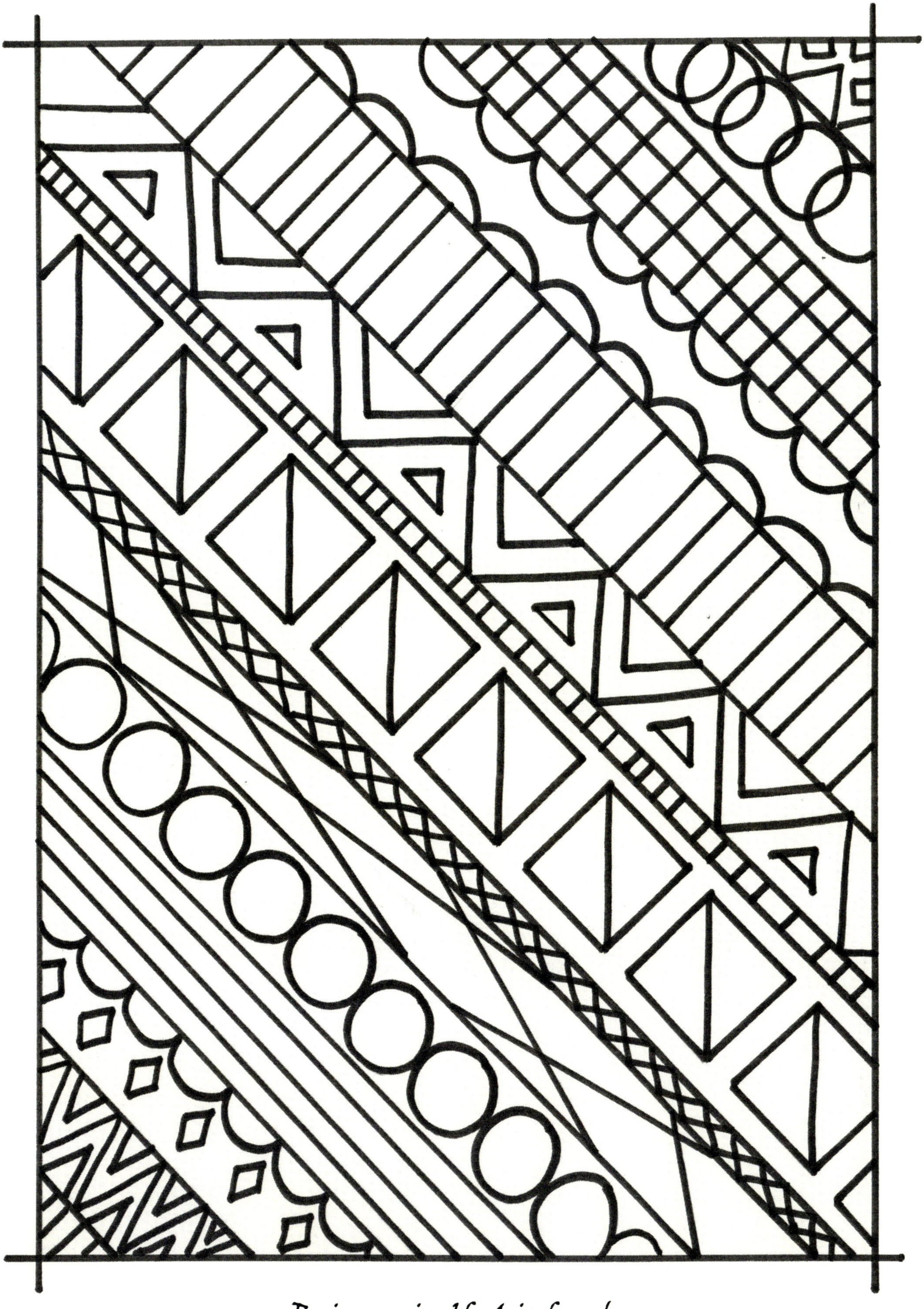

Being mindful is fun!

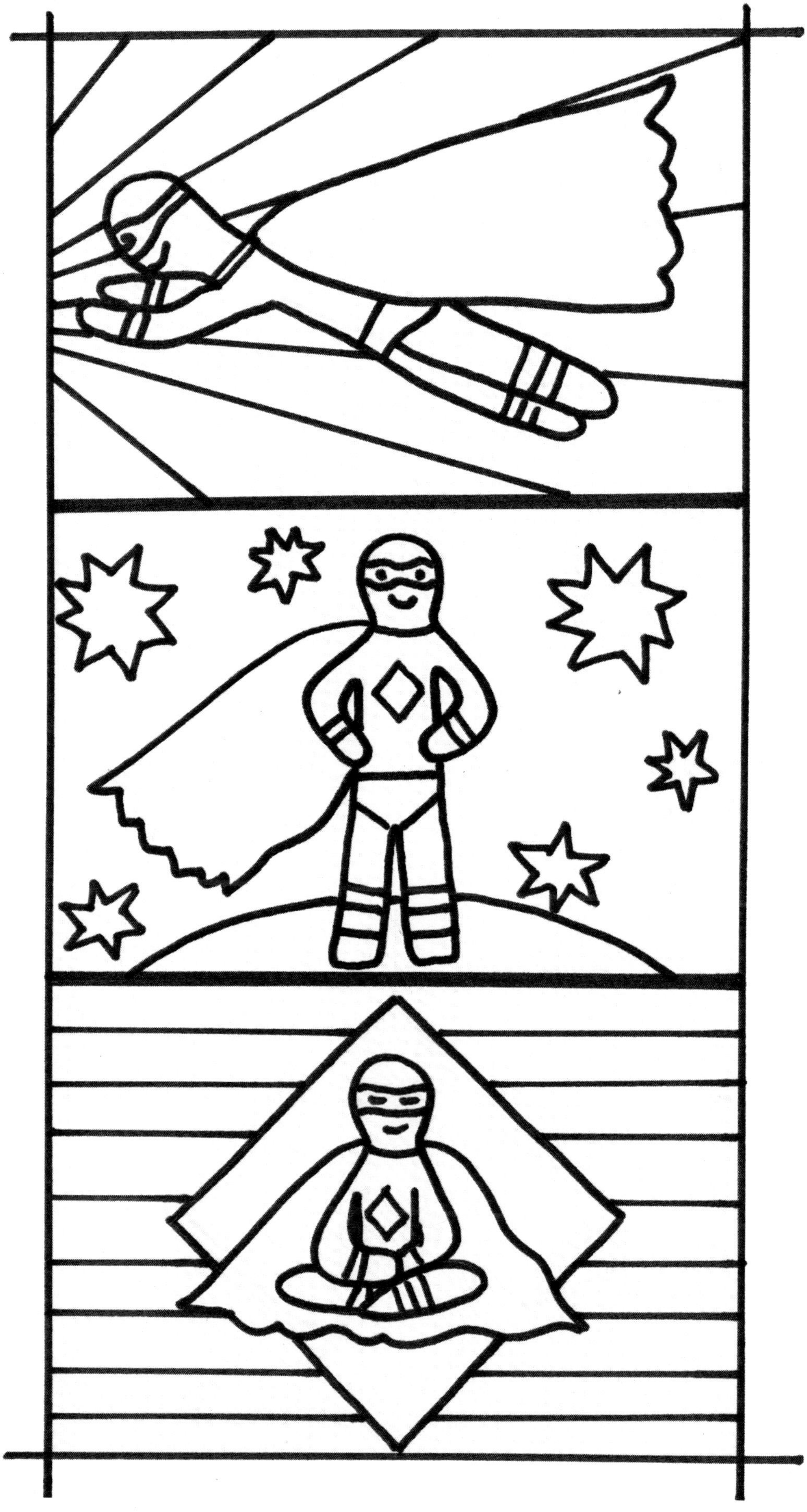

Like a superhero with powers...

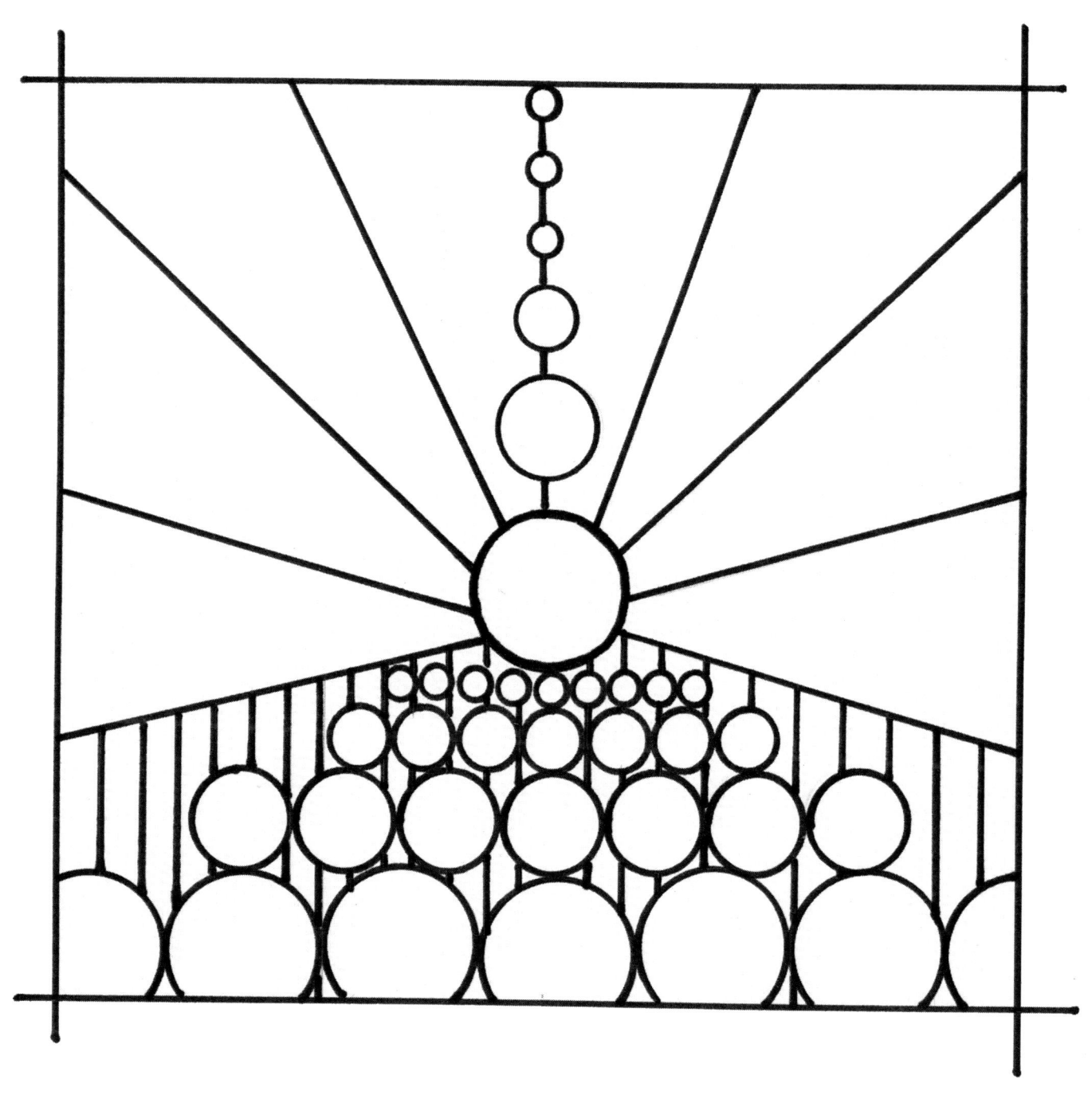

...I can be in control...

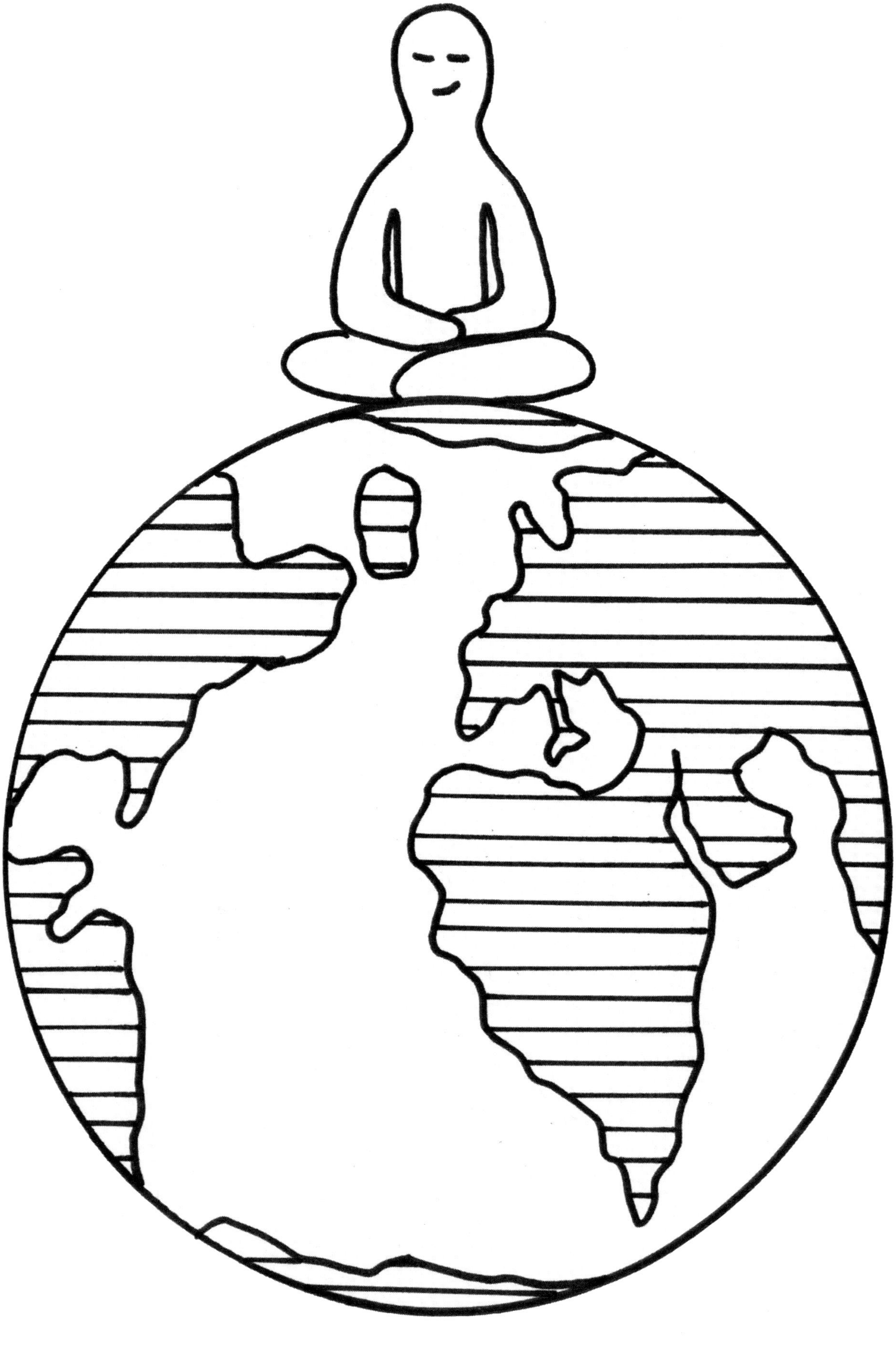

...all places, all hours.

Even if I am mindful...

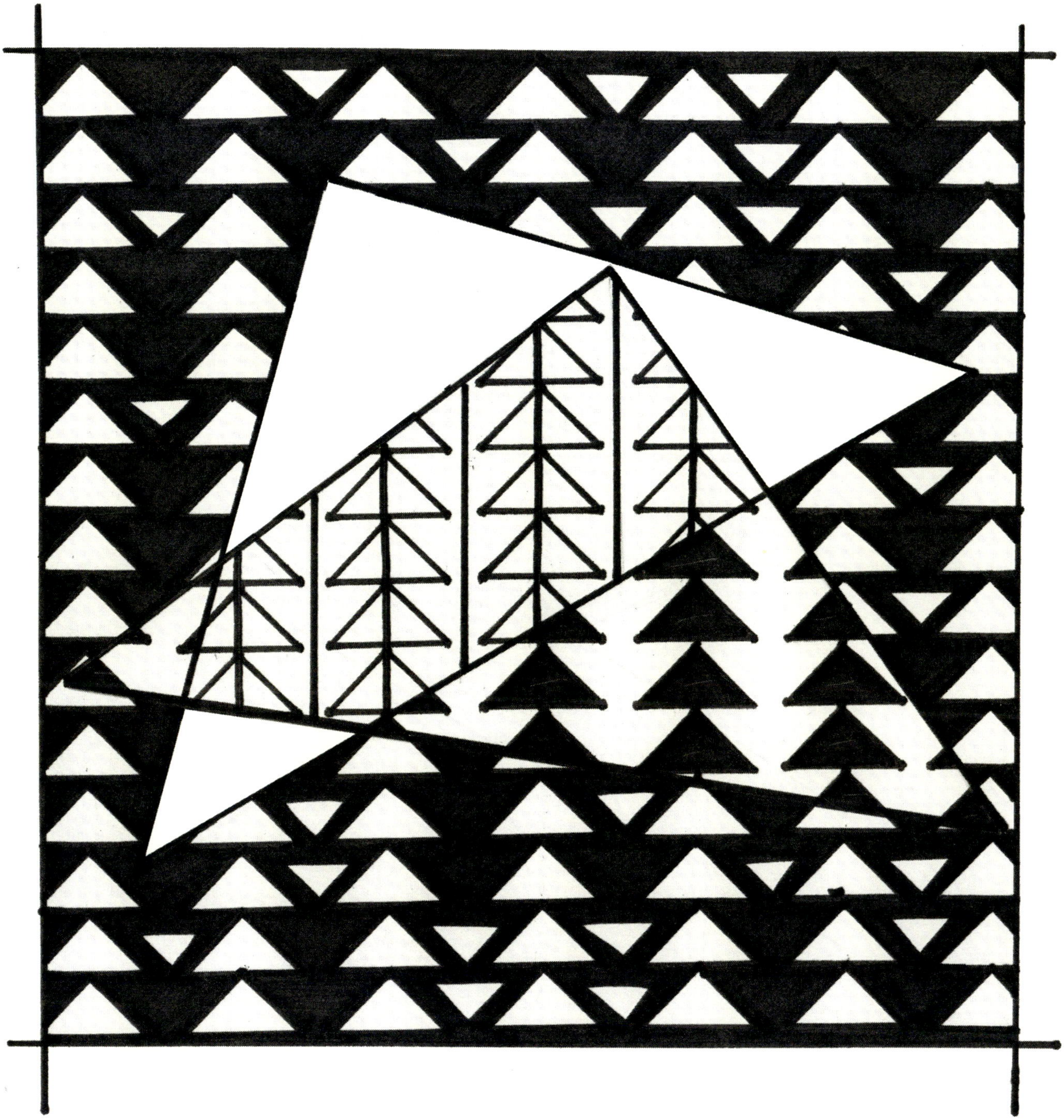

...there will always be times...

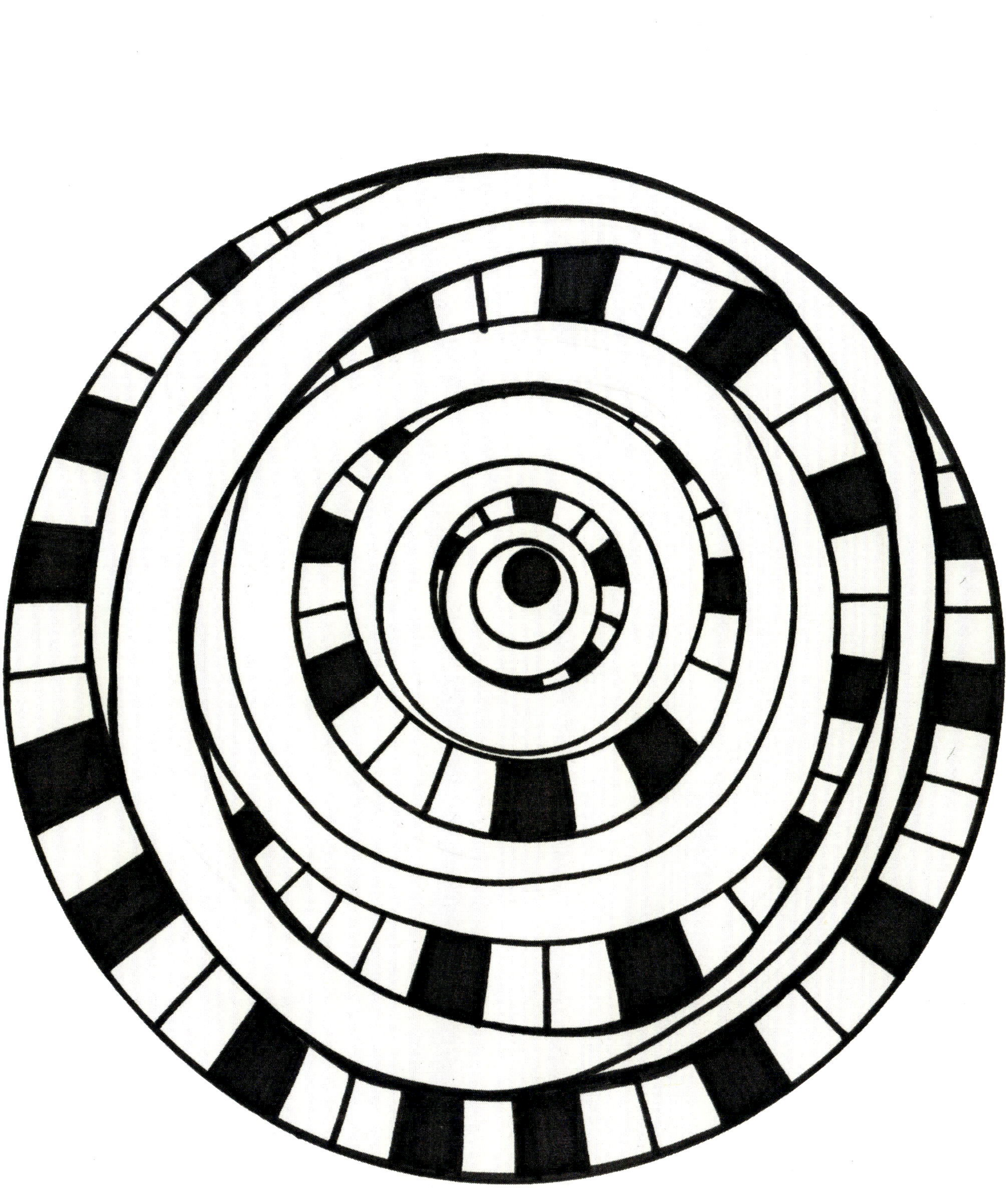

...when it's a little more difficult...

...to observe my mind.

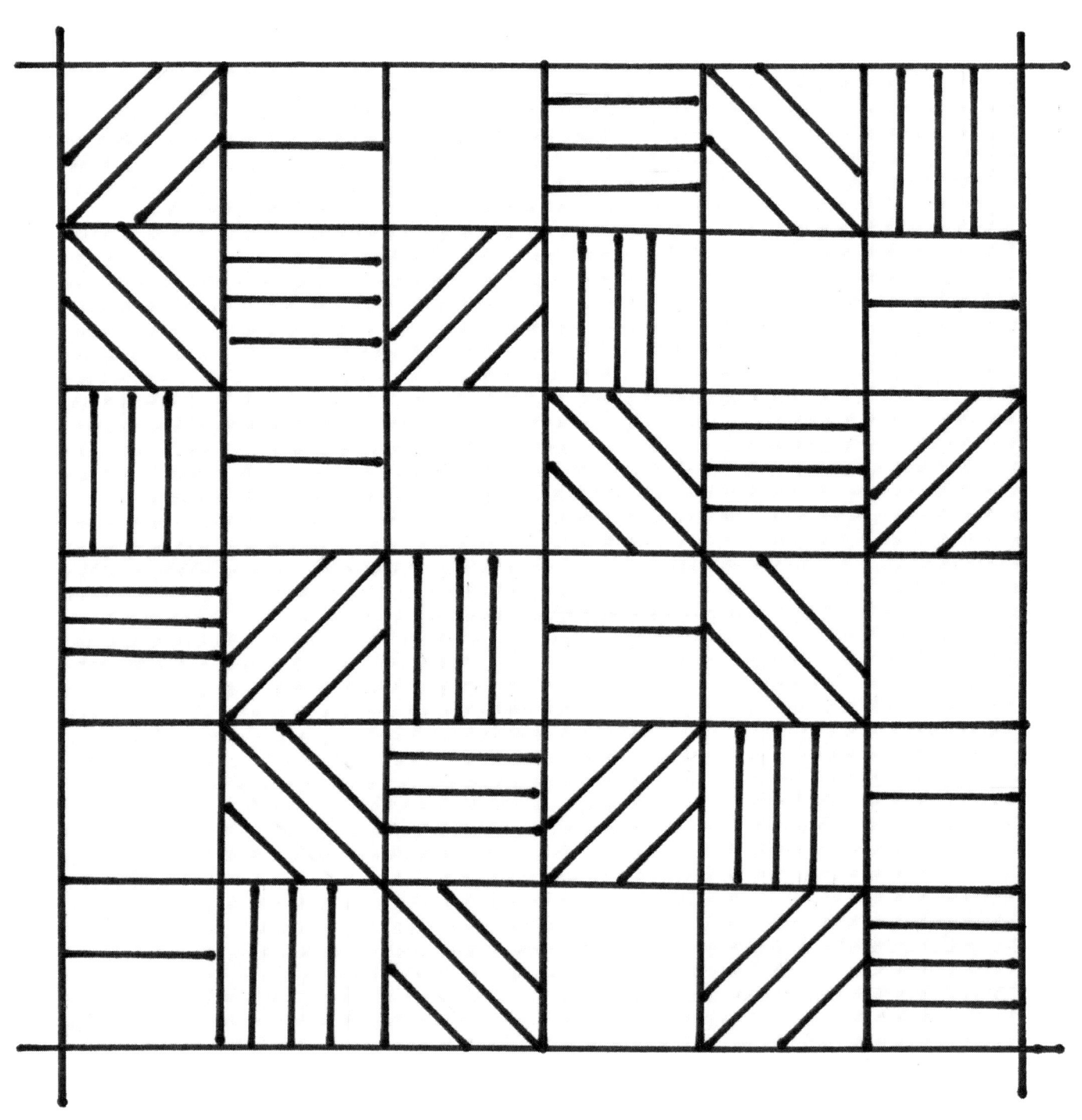

So here is a game...

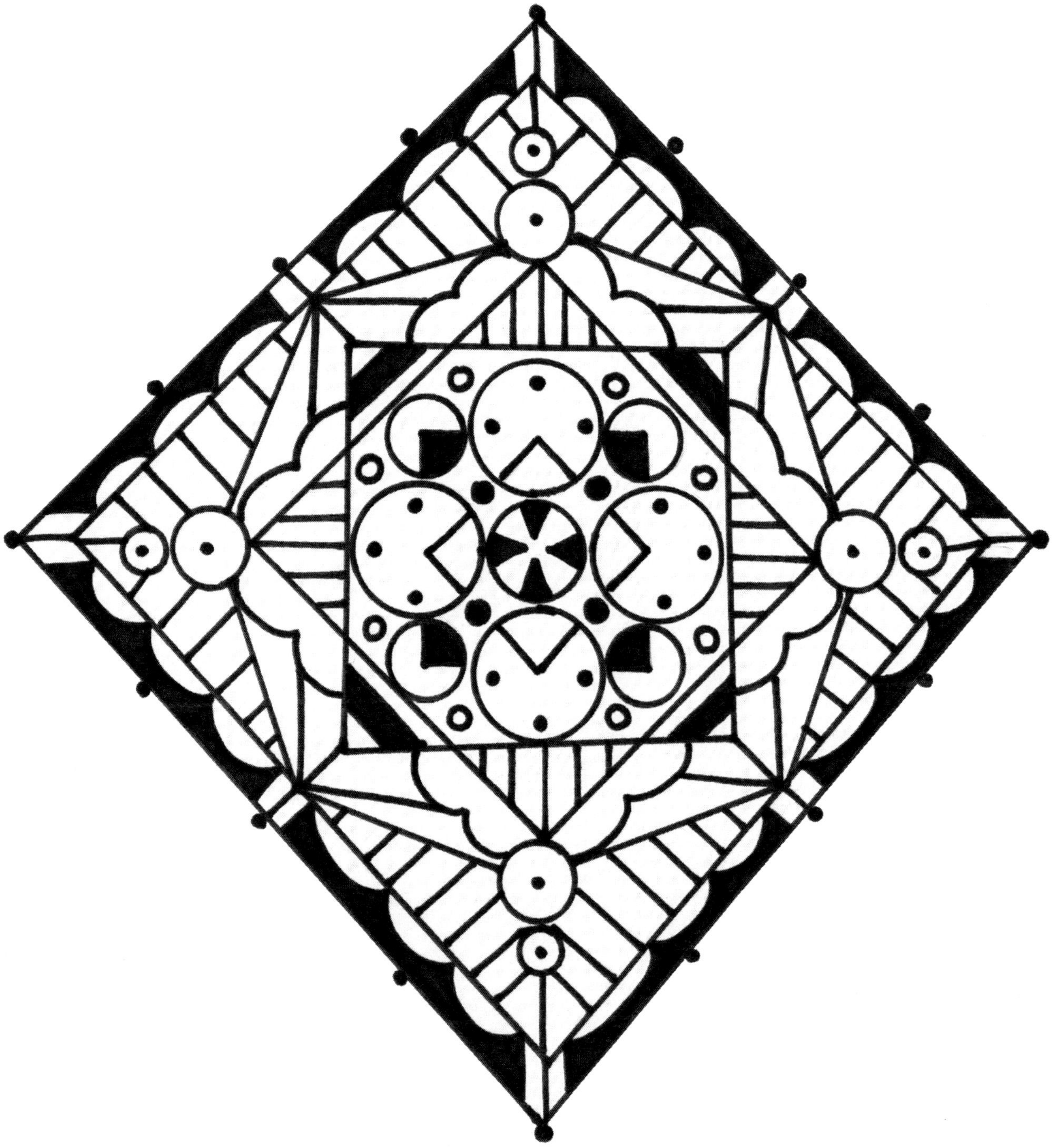

...to change your attitude.

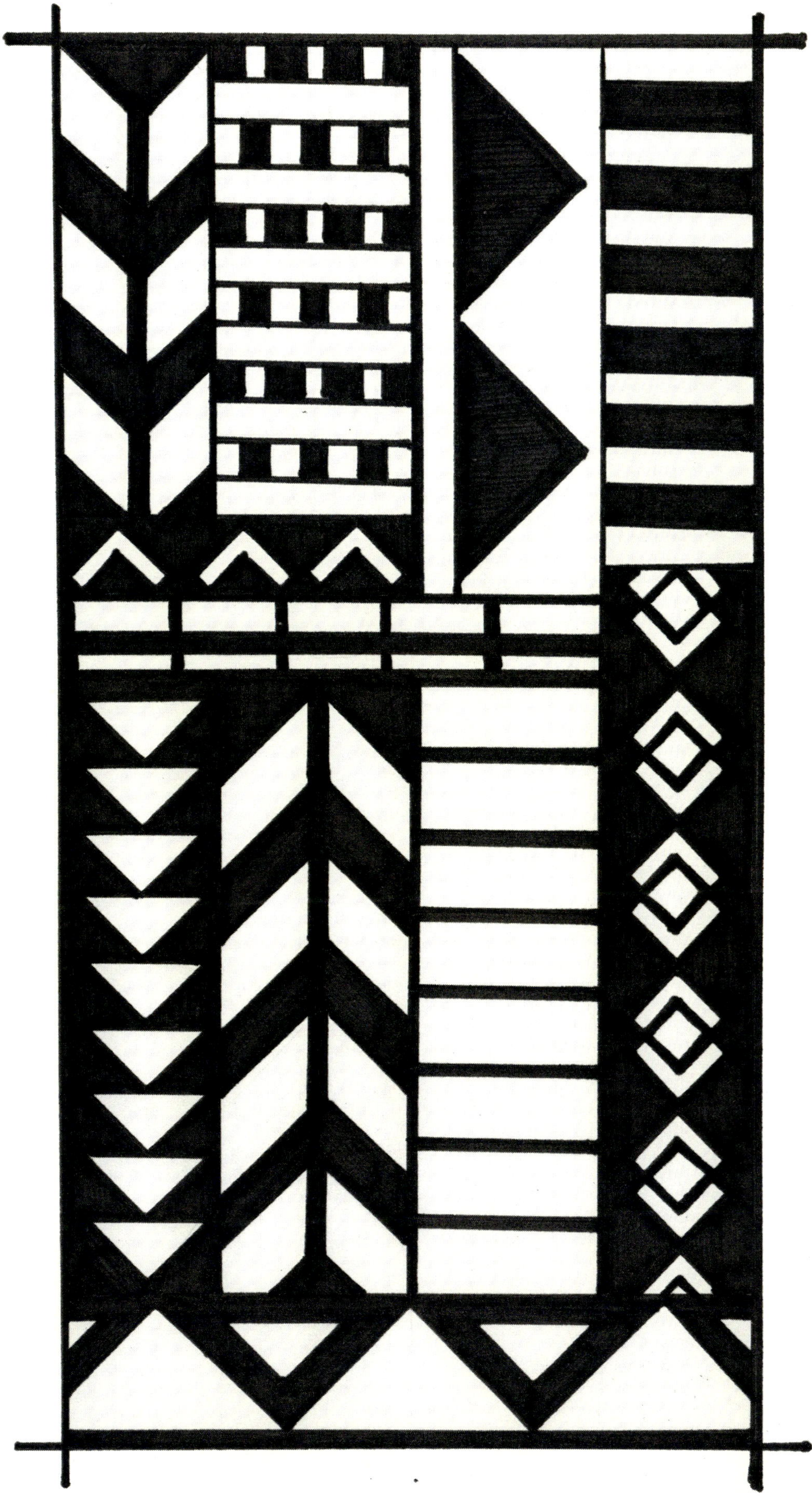

We can do it together...

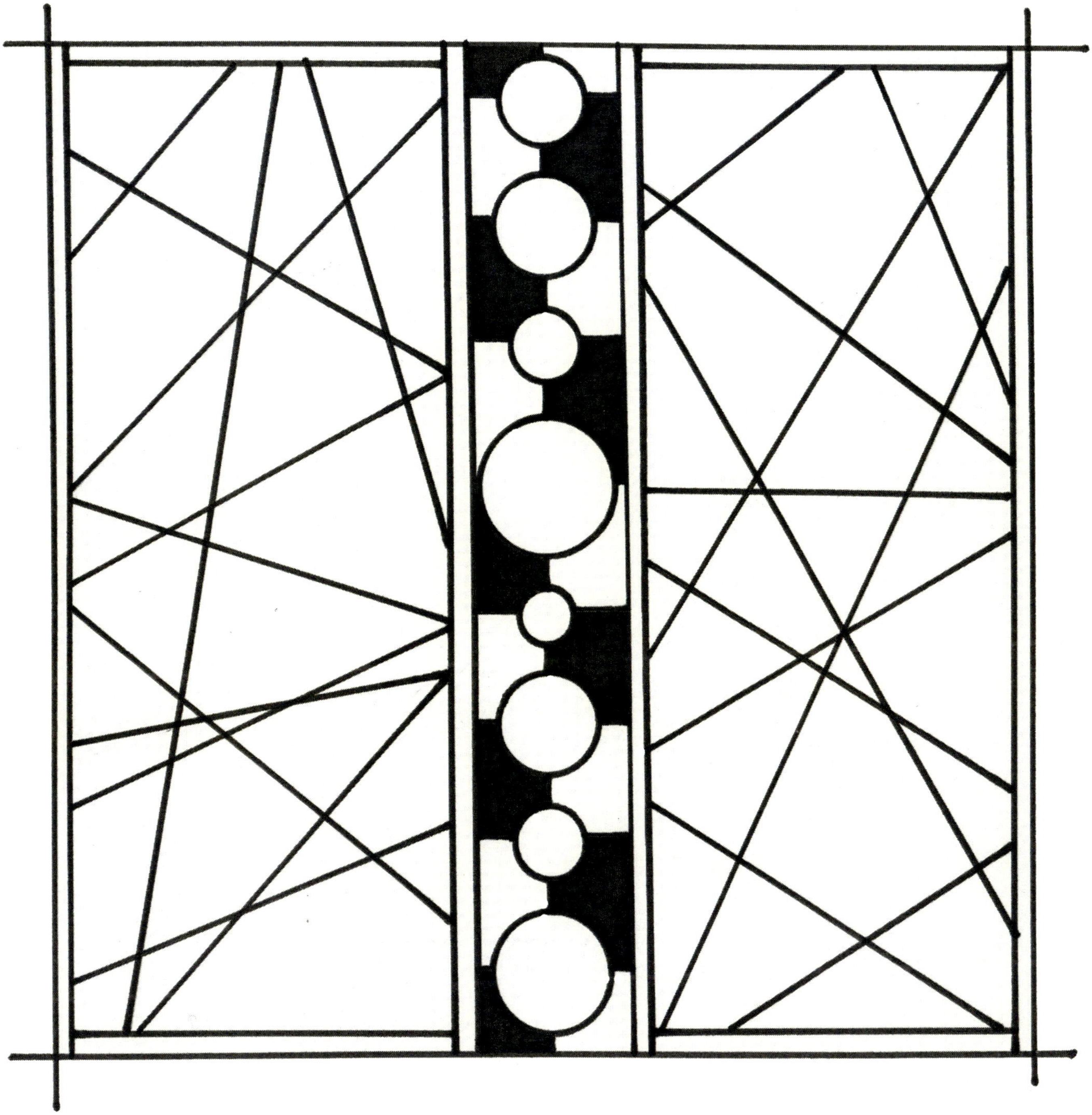

...and feel the gratitude!

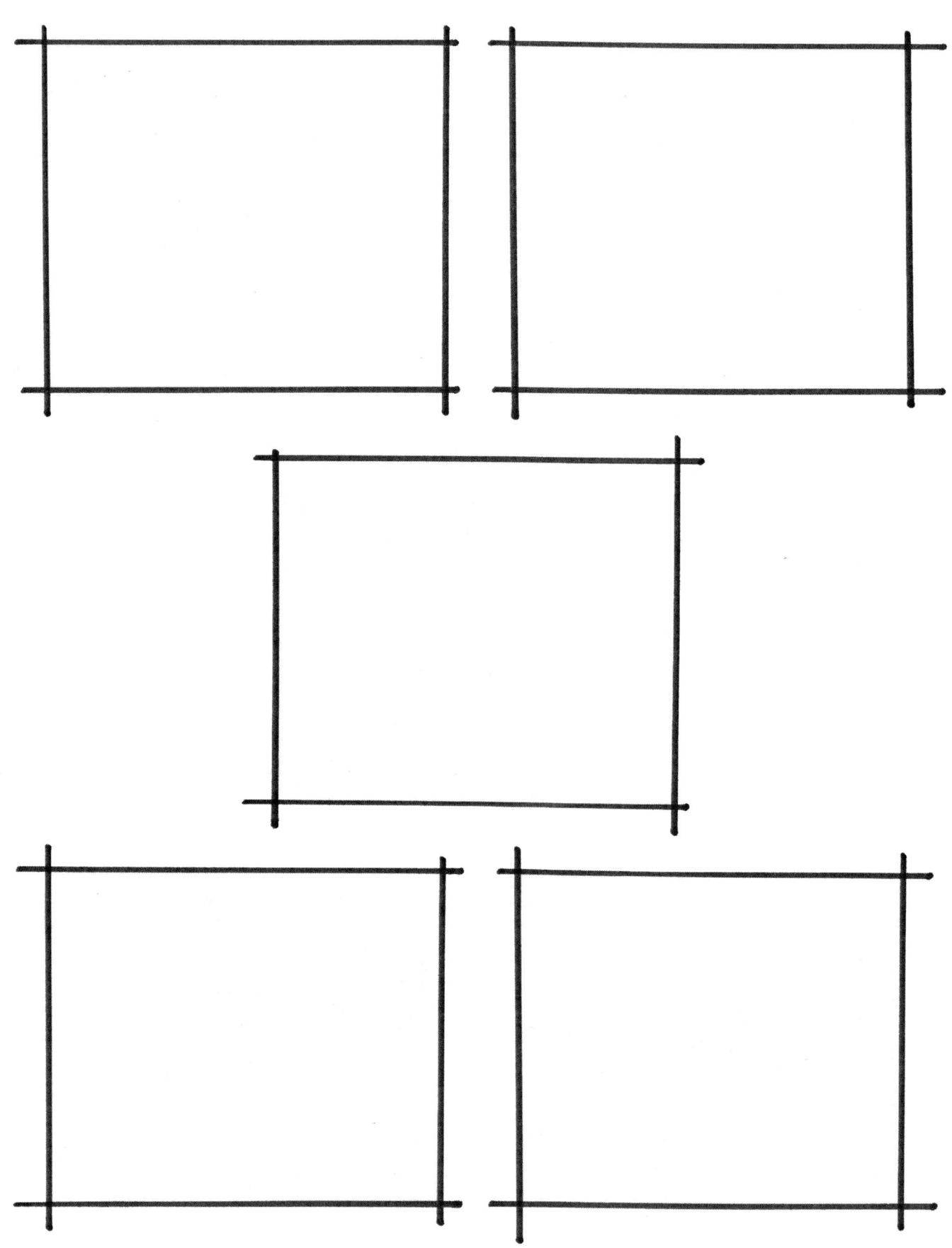

Find five things to TOUCH…go ahead, reach out.

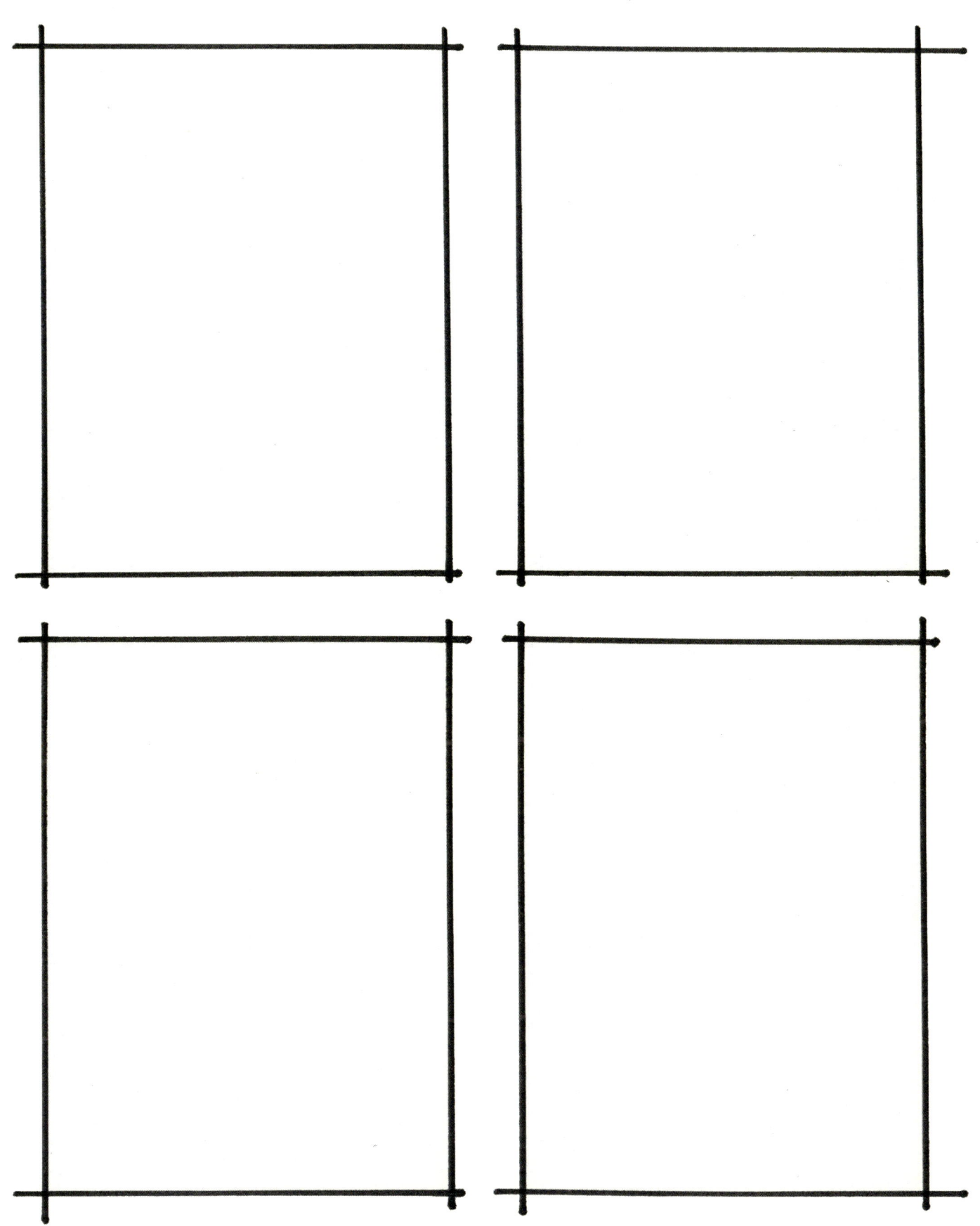

Now four things to SEE...look all about.

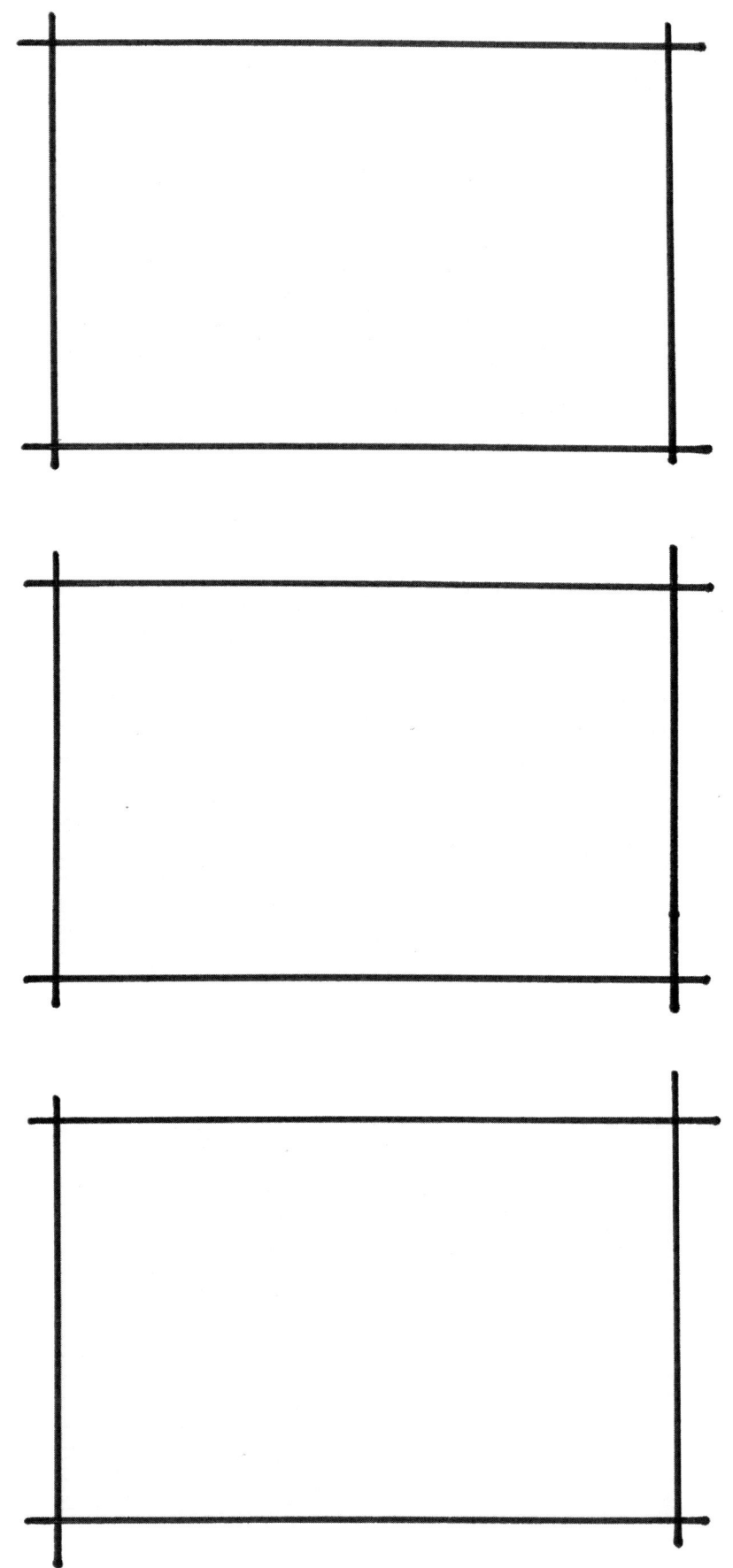

What are three things you HEAR? Pretty or not.

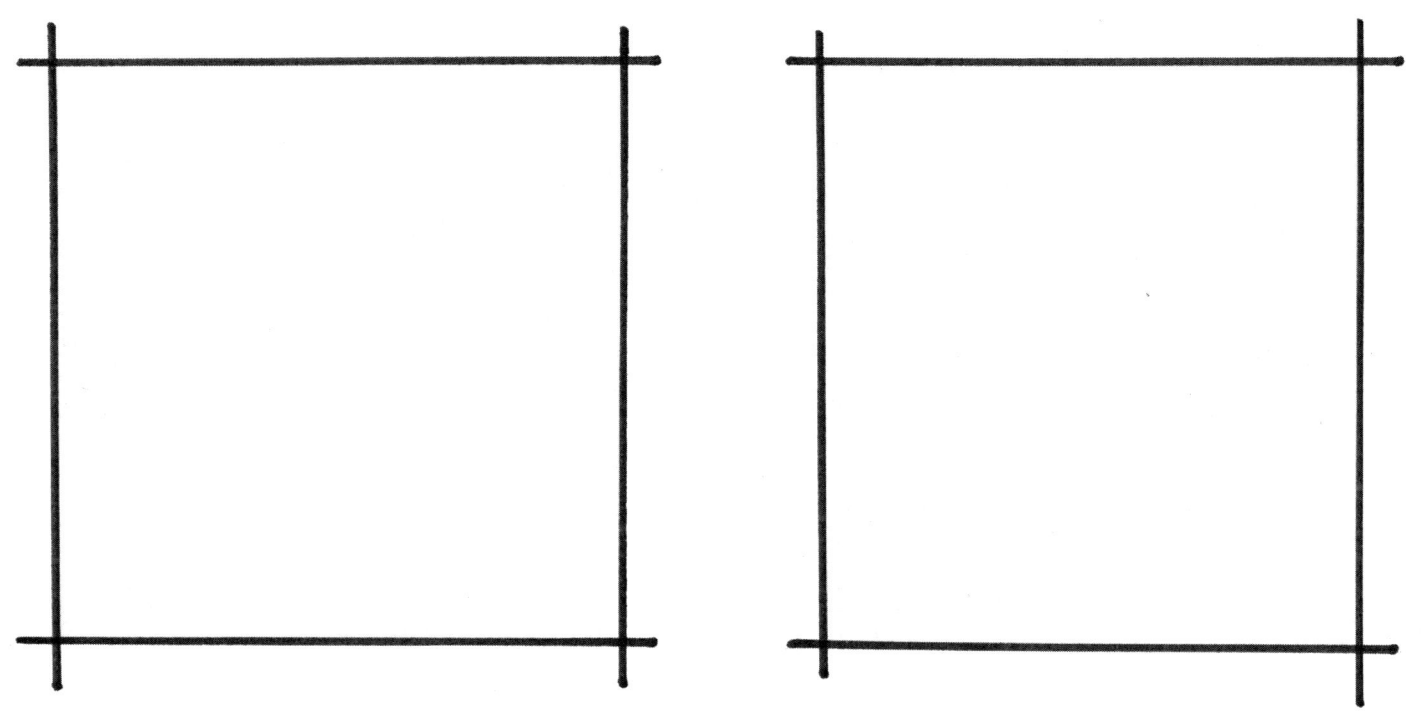

Two things you can SMELL...give it all you've got!

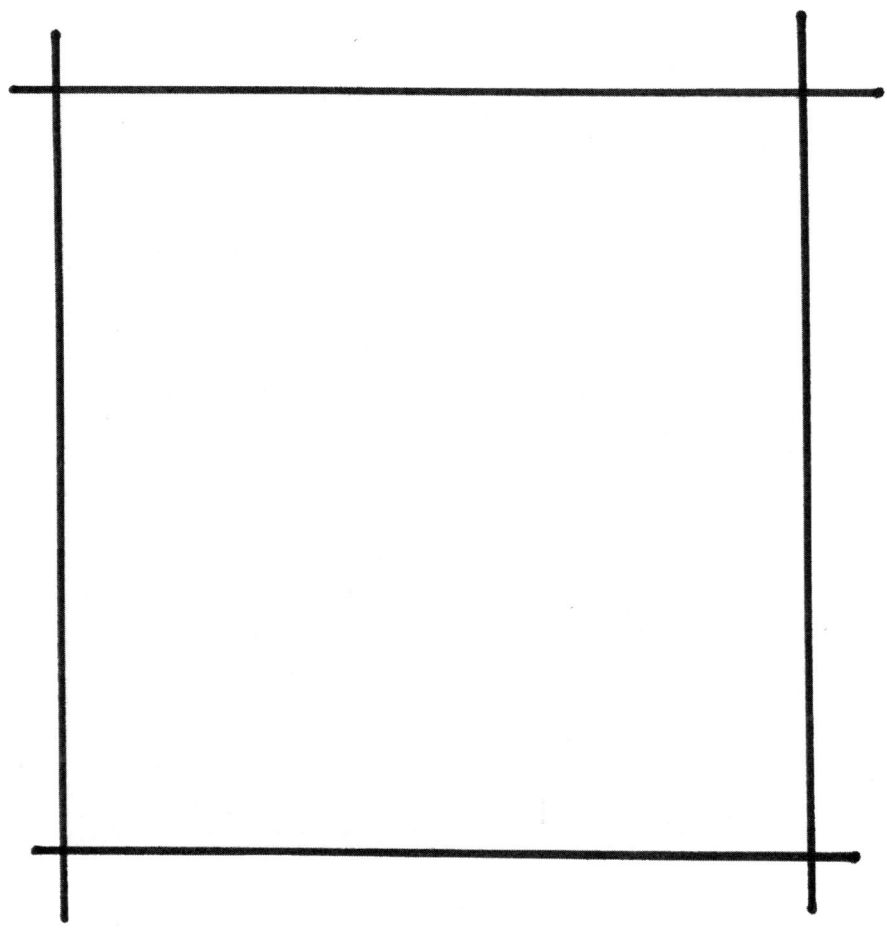

The last one is to TASTE one taste on your tongue...

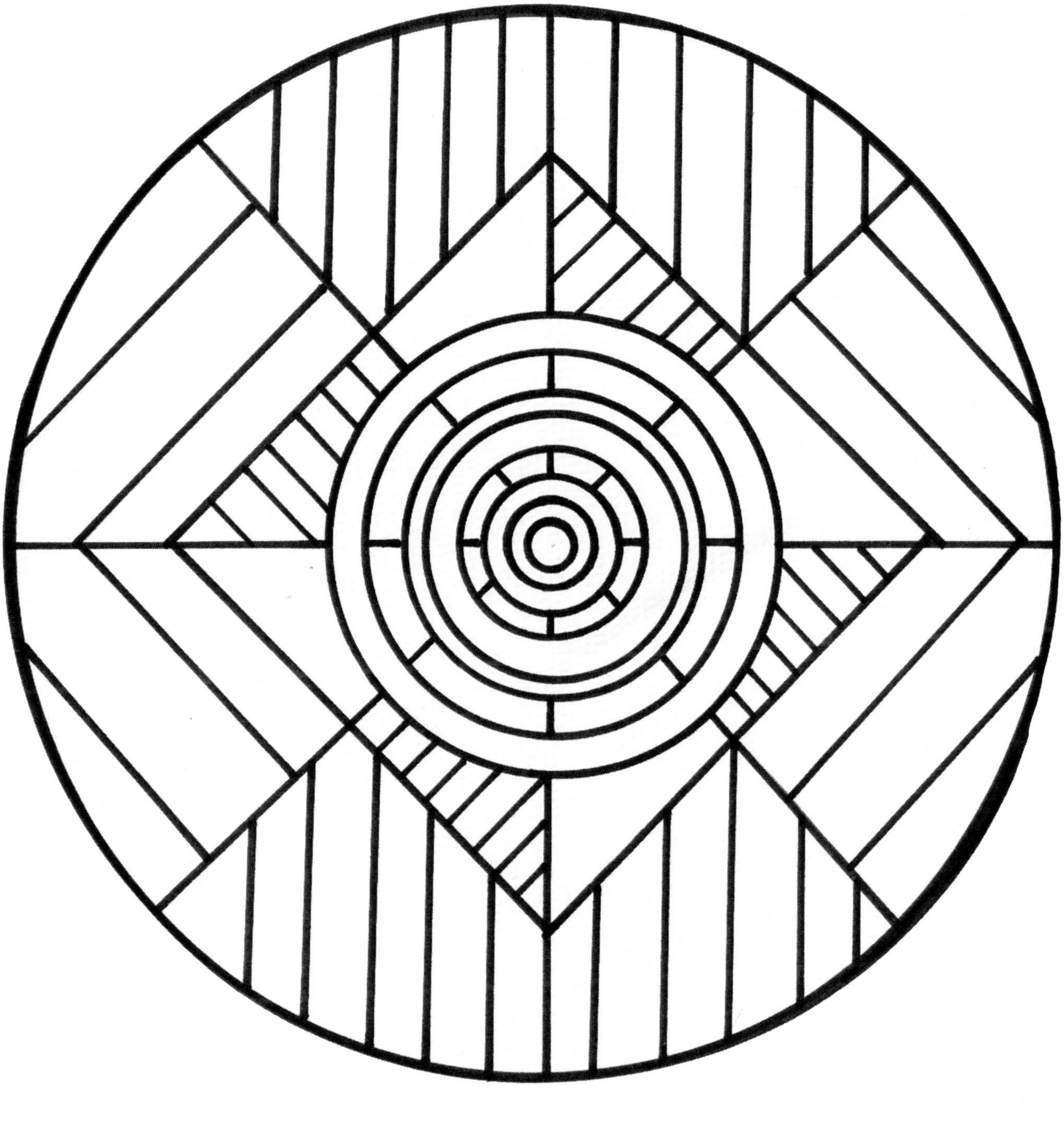

...and now you are grounded...

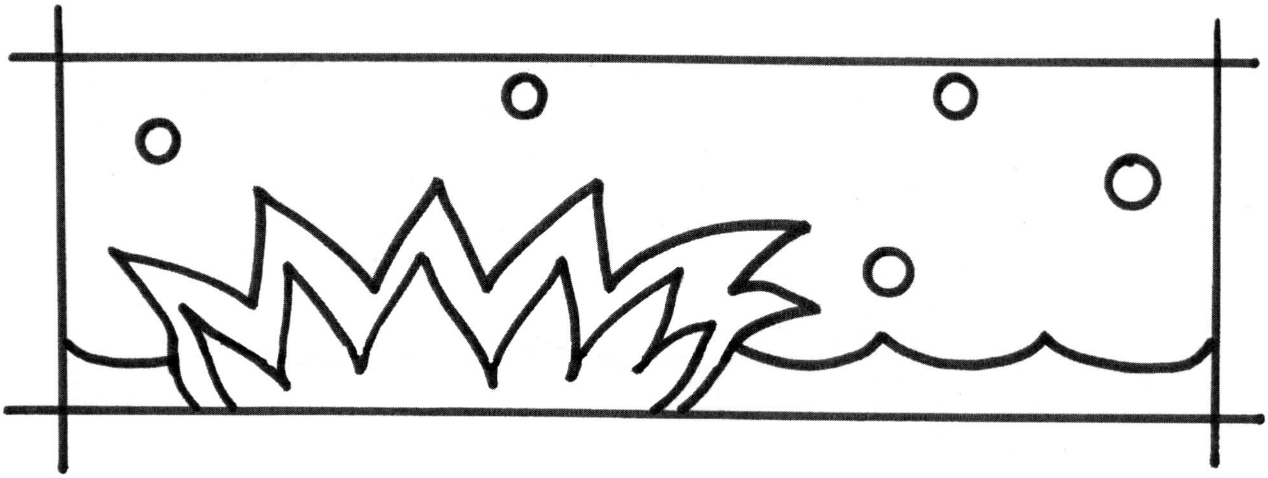

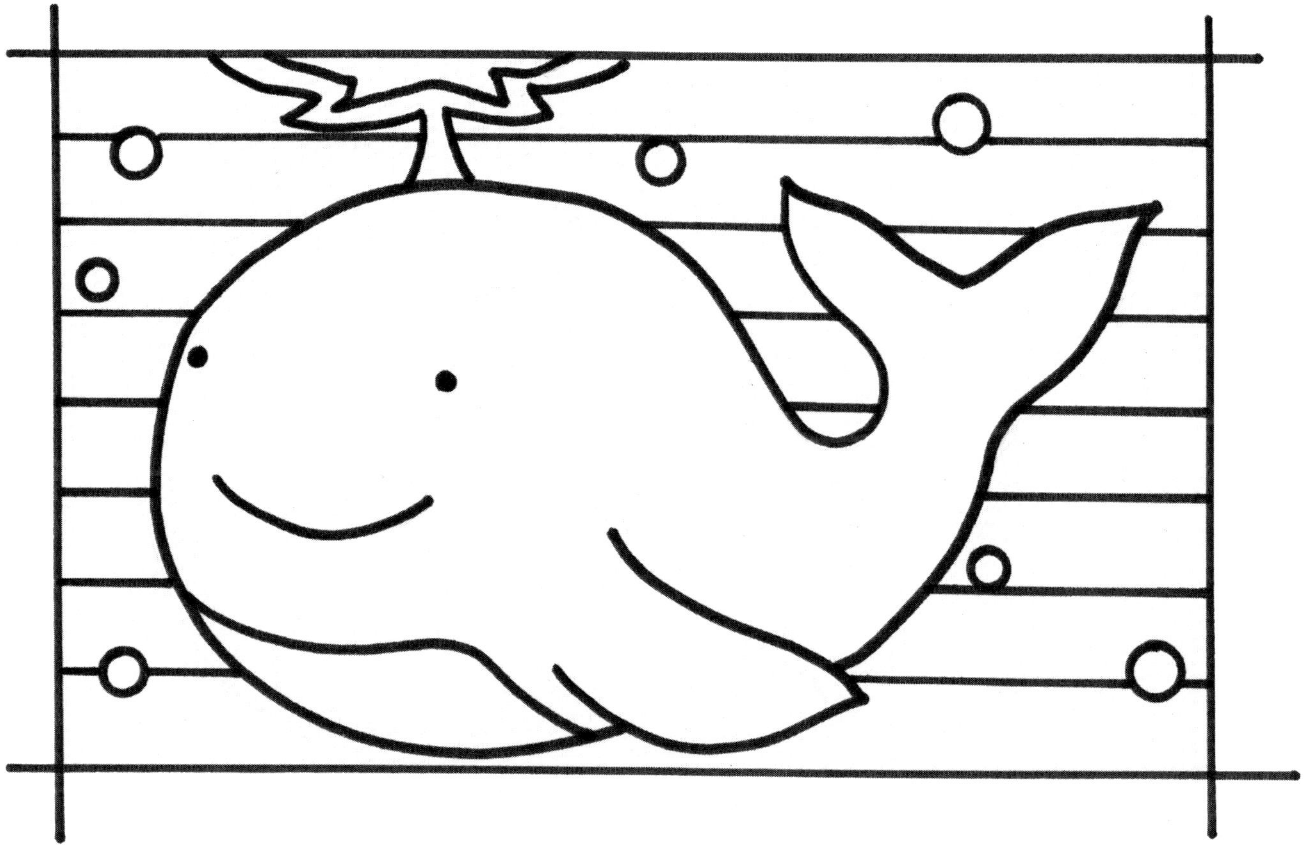

...breathe deeply...

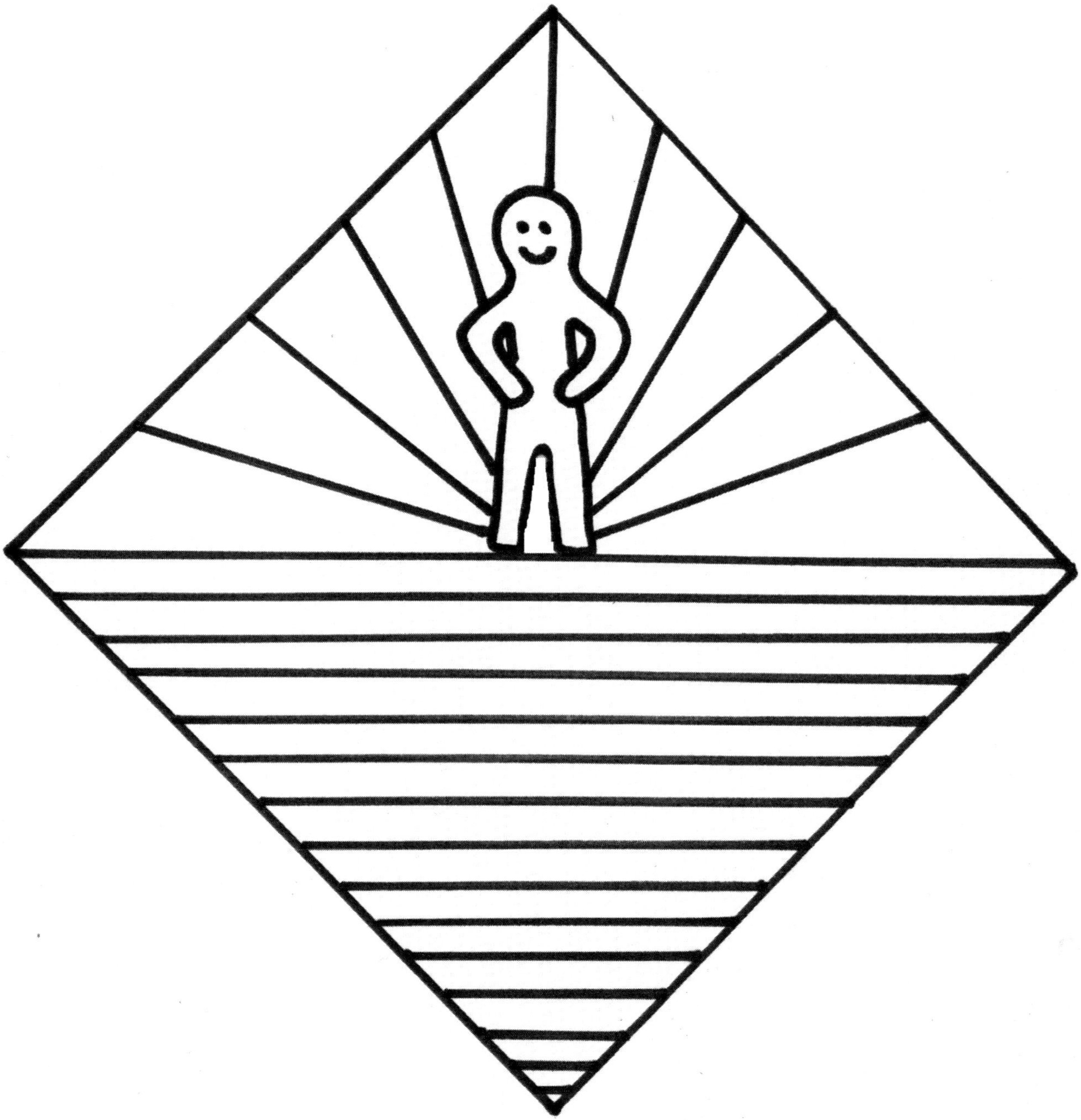

...all one.

I Could Be...Mindful

Now let me see,
What I could be.
I could anything,
That might make my heart sing!

When I can't catch my breath,
When my feelings are large,
When my body is lost,
And emotions are in charge.
I have to remember,
That I hold the key,
The key is called Mindfulness,
And I can practice it easily.

I am a mountain,
My feelings are clouds.
Nothing gets in,
No matter how loud.

I am a surfer,
The waves are emotions.
I sit on my board,
Calmly observing the commotion.

I am a star,
One of many with the name.
A part of it all,
All different, all the same.

I am a flower,
With roots deep in the dirt.
My energy is grounded,
So I feel no hurt.

I am an octopus,
I have sticky feet.
If I need help to focus,
I feel them stick to the street.

I am a rainbow,
I have all the colors.
With sunshine in my heart,
I love myself and others.

I am a lighthouse,
My light does not stray.
The waves pound on my rocks,
But I can always find the way.

Being mindful is fun!
Like a superhero with powers,
I can be in control,
All places, all hours.

Even if I am mindful,
There will always be times,
When it's a little more difficult,
To observe my mind.
So here is a game,
To change your attitude.
We can do it together,
And feel the gratitude.

Find 5 things to touch-go ahead, reach out.

Now 4 things to see-look all about.

What are 3 things you hear? Pretty or not...

And 2 things you can smell-give it all you've got!

The last one is to taste one thing on your tongue.

And now you are grounded,
Breathe deep,
All one.

A Note About Mindfulness

Establishing a mindfulness practice need not be any more complicated than noticing your thoughts or breathing for a few seconds at a time. Any activity during the day, pleasant or not, all provide the perfect opportunity to be mindful: What thoughts are in your head? How do your shoulders feel? What does the air feel like? At any age and in any circumstances, the goal of being present- even for a couple of seconds- is a mindfulness practice that can grow and evolve over time.

As a mother and woman, I have found mindfulness to be such a invaluable tool for myself and my children that I felt compelled to write a book! We use the vocabulary of mindfulness frequently in our home to help navigate both fun and tricky moments. Some of the imagery included in this book are the characters that we use to help visualize the process of conscious observation and energy flow. The concepts are nothing new, and have been used by educators, spiritual leaders and professionals for centuries, particularly in Zen Buddhism. It is my goal to offer a fun and enriching activity book for the whole family whose words and pictures will make the basics of mindfulness clear and useful. While navigating an over-stimulating internal and external world, let us identify our feelings, honor them, and move forward with compassion and love for our fellow beings. I hope you and your family enjoy these pages!

Please enjoy these other titles by Gia Pisto-Reade:

- I Could Be...Color

- I Could Be...Magical Creatures

- The World Tour: A Brief but Thrillingly Informative Introduction to the Sights, Cultures, and Countries of Our World

- How Much Do I Love You?

We would love to hear from you! If you'd like to order more books, send some of your favorite coloring pages, or share your thoughts and experiences, we can be reached at: worldtourbook@gmail.com

For Cyrus, Kaia, and Mia

© 2021 Gia Pisto-Reade "I Could Be Mindful: A Coloring Book" All artwork, text and cover design by Gia Pisto-Reade

ISBN 978-1-7364240-3-2

All rights reserved.